RENNI the RESCUER

Also by Felix Salten

Bambi

RENNI *the* RESCUER

A Dog of the Battlefield

FELIX SALTEN

Translation by KENNETH C. KAUFMAN

Aladdin

New York London Toronto Sydney New Delhi

ALADDIN
An imprint of Simon & Schuster Children's Publishing Division
1230 Avenue of the Americas, New York, NY 10020
First Aladdin paperback edition June 2013

Also available in an Aladdin hardcover edition.
For information about special discounts for bulk purchases, please contact
Simon & Schuster Special Sales at 1-866-506-1949 or
business@simonandschuster.com.
The Simon & Schuster Speakers Bureau can bring authors to your live
event. For more information or to book an event contact the
Simon & Schuster Speakers Bureau at 1-866-248-3049 or
visit our website at www.simonspeakers.com.
Designed by Hilary Zarycky
The text of this book was set in Yana.
Manufactured in the United States of America 0513 OFF
2 4 6 8 10 9 7 5 3 1
Library of Congress Control Number 2012949910
ISBN 978-1-4424-8274-6 (hc)
ISBN 978-1-4424-8273-9 (pbk)
ISBN 978-1-4424-8679-9 (eBook)

RENNI *the* RESCUER

PART I

Chapter I

"WE SHALL CALL HIM RENNI," said the man who raised shepherd dogs, as he took the puppy out of the basket, away from his mother. The old dog raised her head a little and followed her small son with a look of patient resignation.

This was good-bye, and she knew it. But she lay down quietly again and went to sleep—or seemed to go to sleep.

It was not for a dog to resist. She knew that, too. She was trustful and obedient.

To be sure, she still had three of the six puppies, out of the litter born a few days ago. Two had already been taken from her and now the third was going.

The three who were left pressed close against their mother as though asleep and dreaming, but drank eagerly. It gave the mother a feeling of comfort and well-being, and more and more the twilight of drowsiness stole over her.

The man went on speaking. "The last one I give away I always call Renni. I got rid of two yesterday so I won't need to drown any of them. That would be a pity, but I never raise more than three. It keeps the mother in good health and the puppies grow up strong and bright."

Once upon a time in the days of peace this man Vogg had lived near the Adriatic and had raised fox terriers. But after the first World War the confusion of politics and geography had made him very dissatisfied, for he was beginning to grow old, and in the new order of things he found no order at all. Since he could not accustom himself to surroundings which had become uncongenial he had moved northward and settled in a country which had been spared the alarms of war and had remained unchanged. He did not like changes.

He did not take into account that he had changed his own residence. And the fact that he was now raising shepherd dogs instead of terriers hardly seemed a change. He was still raising dogs, as he had always done. He had a kennel, and so life went on much as it had gone on before.

It was time anyhow to stop breeding fox terriers; there were too many of them. They had become commonplace, ladies' playthings, almost a kind of toilet article; they were inbred and too apt to go mad. So he began to raise shepherds–more commonly known as "police dogs"–a breed he loved and understood. He could not live without dogs.

"Now, of course, you will have to feed him with a bottle for several weeks," the man said to George, "and then he may have rice cooked in milk. You must raise him to like vegetables and fruit. Mix a little bone meal with his food, and for the first year go easy with meat."

George smiled and took the tiny Renni in his arms. A sort of warm, milky fragrance rose from the basket where the mother lay with her children. A healthy dog-smell filled the whole kennel.

"I'm not going to give you his pedigree now," said the man. "I'll wait and see how Renni turns out."

"Why should I have a pedigree?"

George pressed the little brown-black bundle of wool against him and Renni gave a soft whimper. It was a thin and tiny sound, almost like the twittering of a bird. He seemed to be feebly seeking something. George stuck his finger into the puppy's mouth, and felt the hot, thirsty, eager sucking. It made him happy.

"I've always wanted a dog," he said. "Thank you."

"Don't forget, his name is Renni," Vogg called after him.

"Renni, good old Renni," George kept saying on the way home, and there was a world of love in his tone.

George was a sturdy, good-natured fellow not yet thirty. He lived with his mother in a neat little house in a big garden near the city. The surrounding field was his, too. He raised flowers, cabbages, lettuce, and tomatoes, and sold them on the market.

Now he was going home very, very proud of this helpless creature that belonged to him. He would see to it that this little thing grew up into a noble dog, useful, of service to the world. Yes, indeed, that would be worth while.

His mother laughed when she caught sight of Renni. Mother Marie laughed most of the time. She had a very cheerful disposition and made George's home life happy.

"Do you want me to raise this youngster?" she asked.

"No!" George had no intention of giving his mother extra work. He would do it all himself and take great pleasure in it, too. He began filling the bottle with warm milk. "Not too hot and not too cool," warned his mother. "It ought to be just at body heat."

"Yes," agreed George, "but at puppy heat." His face wore a comical expression of superior wisdom as he put the nipple on the bottle.

"Jealous!" said his mother.

"I am that," admitted George, holding the food out to Renni.

Renni tried to stand, sprawled. His thick clumsy legs refused to hold his weight. Collapsed on his stomach, he drank greedily. Mother Marie brought in an old basket lined with rags and soft old cloths. "I wonder if he will sleep in here with Kitty."

"Why, of course," George assured her.

"He's almost too young to know anything. He's still almost blind. The question is how Kitty will act toward her new bedfellow."

Kitty was Mother Marie's young kitten. She was perhaps four weeks older than Renni. They had started calling to her, Kitty! Kitty! and since she had learned to come to this call it seemed perfectly natural to let that be her name. So they never thought of giving her another.

"How would you expect her to act?" George wanted to know. "Kitty hasn't had any experience yet. It will be perfectly all right with her."

Mother Marie was doubtful. "What about her inborn hate of dogs, her natural instinct?"

"I don't believe in any such thing." George was very positive. "That hate you speak of is just a result of human cruelty. Nothing but thoughtless human cruelty has made cats and dogs hate each other."

"Well, we can try it," conceded Mother Marie. She called, "Kitty! Kitty!"

George put the puppy to bed in the basket. Renni had drunk all he could hold. Now he was whimpering softly, not in pain but with a sort of yearning. He moved his head slowly as if it were too heavy to lift.

"He's missing his mother's warm body," said George. "It's just too bad. And he misses his brothers and sisters."

"Kitty, where are you?" called Mother Marie. "Of course Mr. Renni must be kept nice and warm. Here, come on, Kitty."

The kitten, grey and white, tiger-striped, came up mincing daintily, her eyes wide with curiosity, and quite ready for war.

"No nonsense now, and don't be coy," commanded Mother Marie. She picked Kitty up from the floor, pressed the soft body against her chin, blew on the silky fur and put her in the basket.

Kitty, arching her back a little, smelled Renni over carefully and curiously. For a moment things hung in the balance. Then she lay down beside him with a graceful sort of movement as much as to say, "This is all right with me."

Renni had no more than felt her presence there when he cuddled up quite close. He stopped whimpering. He only sighed once or twice, deeply and comfortably. Kitty put one paw caressingly on his neck. She began purring almost at once. They fell asleep side by side.

"Cat and dog, together," smiled Mother Marie.

George nodded his satisfaction. "I knew it! What about that natural instinct now?"

Chapter II

IT WAS NOT LONG BEFORE RENNI OUTgrew the bottle, and the basket soon became too small for him, but he shared his new bed with Kitty and ate his milk and rice out of the same dish with her. He liked the world about him, the rooms and the garden, and he would no more have given up the kitten than she him.

For hours at a time the two would roll over each other in good-natured play. Renni's thick clumsy paw would bowl Kitty over. Then he would stand above her and mouth at her head, nip her with his needle-like teeth, or with his swiftly lapping tongue would wash her face, neck and breast.

Kitty would lie on her back and lash out at him, boxing his ears with lightning-swift paws. It did not hurt at all, even when her hind legs played a tattoo on his stomach. When she got tired of the game up she would get, and in a flash leave Renni dumbfounded. Light as a feather she would land on top of a dresser, or, if she were out in the garden, she would shoot up a tree.

Climbing a tree was one thing Renni could not do. He knew he couldn't and he didn't even want to try. But every time Kitty did it, the feat left him astounded.

Renni was a funny-looking fellow. His skin hung in loose folds like a coat too big for him and swelled out on his forehead into puffs and wrinkles that gave him an expression positively sorrowful. His ears were large, out of all proportion to his size, and they stuck up stiff and sharp from his head. To even the slightest noise they seemed to answer, "I hear you." Black hair covered his back like a saddlecloth and made smudges across his face. The edges of his lips glistened deep black. Even his gums were black. But his neck, breast and the underside of his body glowed with tawny yellow like a lion's skin.

His tail, not yet completely plumed did not roll but hung down in a slight curve. It resembled nothing so much as a black toy broom.

He had not yet gained full use of his thick clumsy legs. Often he would fall all over himself and seem to be trying to show off, like a circus clown. But not for one minute did he really think of showing off or of impressing anyone; everything funny that he did was quite unintentional. He was not the least bit stupid. It was just that the world was so new to him and he was so new to himself.

His whole appearance was as awkward as his actions. There was something absolutely childlike in Renni, but the charm of the future was in him, too, and the promise of a later beauty.

On the other hand, the kitten had all the grace of early perfection. The complete charm of youth was hers, the magic of an abundant energy that spread cheerfulness and joy in play. Though Renni was the stronger, Kitty was the leader, with her supple spirit and her genius for getting into things. Renni followed her lead as a matter of course.

Kitty loved to sharpen her claws. She would attack the cloth of the curtains, the sofa, the armchairs, stretching her body, tearing great holes.

Renni had to try his needle-like teeth on everything hard. He would gnaw slippers, shoes, the edge of benches. He would fall eagerly and blissfully on every object he could possibly reach.

Mother and son had quite a problem with these tendencies, but managed to deal with them without losing their good humour. Mother Marie hung old rags all over the house for Kitty, and George gave Renni dog biscuits made in the shape of bones to gnaw on. It filled him with delight to see the two young animals always so gay and so active.

They never had the remotest idea of resorting to punishment. Mother Marie knew just how useless it is to punish a cat. "Cats are wild animals," she would always say, "free, untamed and untamable. If you want their friendship you must let them go their own way. The only reason cats live with people is so they can be more comfortable. If they ever become attached to anyone it is by their own free choice. They don't know the meaning of obedience, and we simply have no right to expect it of them."

Ordinarily Mother Marie did not have much to say. It was only when she got on this cat theory of hers that she turned loose at a great rate, as if she expected someone to contradict her. But George had no idea of contradicting. He agreed with it all absolutely.

Mother Marie would make another point: "People have been spoiled by the servility of dogs, and they're so stupid they don't like cats because cats know how to stick up for themselves. Yes, indeed, if there's one thing people can't endure in other people, let alone in animals, it is independence."

George was willing to admit this too. He would not even take issue over the servility of dogs, but when his mother stopped talking he would begin to lay down some ideas of his own. He thought it horrible and cowardly for a man to punish a dog.

"A dog," he said, "is smart enough to get upset by a serious scolding and feel remorse." Now in turn his mother would agree with him. She did not raise the slightest objection, and thus there was always peace in the house. Both of them knew these speeches pretty well by heart. Each heard them often from the other. They were patient, mother and son. They were as united and loyal as parent and child always ought to be but very seldom are.

One day Renni began to bark for the first time. His voice wavered from a high, keen whining to a deep resonant tone and back again. Renni was sounding the alarm. A strange dog, a Doberman pinscher, had caught sight of Kitty and, ready for battle, was coming through the open lattice gate from the street into the garden. Kitty arched her back like a "U" upside down, remained rooted to the spot and looked defiantly into the pinscher's eyes.

Renni was yapping excitedly, for he had never seen

either an arched back or a strange dog. Very likely he had supposed he was the only dog in the world.

The pinscher paid no attention to Renni. Coming close with his feet bent for a leap, he growled threateningly at the cat and waited for the moment to seize her. He waited in vain. Suddenly Kitty flashed her sharp claws into his face. The pinscher drew back, and swift as lightning Kitty was up in the top of an apple tree. The angry pinscher began barking up the tree. Renni was all excitement. Amazed at the pinscher, he barked now in his funny, squeaky, puppy voice, now in the deep bass of a police dog. He felt just as big a dog as the other. It was a regular dog-duet.

Kitty from the safe height of her treetop listened to the hullabaloo with the utmost peace of soul. Then George ran up and chased the pinscher out of the garden to his master who had been calling him in vain. When the gate had clapped to, the pinscher, as if to show contempt for banishment, hoisted his leg. Then he dashed madly after his master.

It took a long time for Renni to quiet down. Kitty

came down from her tree as calmly as though nothing had happened, but she did not seem to want to play. Very carefully and deliberately she made her toilet and then she lay down in the sunshine. Renni, perfectly agreeable to this or anything else, stretched out by her side.

Using this incident as a text, Mother Marie and George might well have aired their opinions about cats, dogs and human beings, but they had done so a short time before and they had the sense not to do so again. They knew how to be moderate in all things.

The episode of the pinscher wrought a change in Renni. He had become acquainted with the garden gate; he had found out that beyond it the street stretched out forever. People strode along it. Dogs ran swiftly or prowled slowly past. Sometimes they would stop to investigate the gate, turn around sniffing three or four times in the same place before they finally made up their minds, and then, with a serious or even worried expression, would lift their legs.

For Renni, the street was a place of charm and mystery. All sorts of fascinating, enticing smells made their way inside, through the garden fence; it was enough to put his head in a whirl. As occasion offered he would slip out unknown to everyone and soon be striking up peaceful acquaintance with strange dogs. He was initiated into the mysteries of trailing, of mutual sniffings, into the ceremony of lifting the leg properly–all of which he observed formally and to the letter.

When he found he could not get back into the garden because the gate was closed, he would sit whimpering pitifully. George would let him in. "Renni," he would say sadly, reproachfully, "Renni, you know you must not go out on the street alone. You're not allowed to do that. You'll turn out a good-for-nothing vagabond. You might get stolen. You might get run over. There's nothing out there that concerns you at all. Do you hear? Nothing at all!"

Crouching down or lying on his back, his paws in the air, Renni would listen piously to this sermon, apparently filled with remorse.

Still Renni had a notion that there was a good deal

outside which did concern him, and so he had an adventure that came within a hair's breadth of costing him his life. Once more he ran out on the street, loitered around on the pavement, chased after a dog and found himself across the way where the fields spread out. He was so tantalized by the smells of mice and moles that he went rummaging about here and there.

George, who had been trying to keep an eye on him in vain, at last caught sight of him. "Renni," he cried, "Renni, come here this minute!"

But Renni did not come. No matter how loud George called, Renni seemed to have forgotten his name completely, forgotten that George had anything to do with him, But at last something of the sort must have entered his head, and he started back.

George was happy when he saw this and cried out, "Good boy! That's a fine dog!" though the puppy did not deserve such praise at all. But then a strange spell came over Renni. He lay down right in the middle of the highway. He lay there deaf to all shouts.

Nobody could ever determine whether some sudden pain caused him to stretch out that way, or whether he grew tired, or whether he lay down to think over the riddle of the universe.

Whichever it was, he did not get a chance to carry out his purpose. He did not have time to make up his mind about anything. A truck came roaring along straight at Renni. Choking with fear and anguish, all George could do was utter a dull moan. It was too late to get Renni, too late now to call him again.

Renni did not move. He acted as though the thunder of the heavy truck meant no more to him than the buzzing of a fly.

George tried hard to signal the driver of the threatening monster, but the driver seemed as much a monster as the truck. George's wild and anguished warning had not the slightest effect on him. George grew rigid, felt helpless. It came to him now that the driver could not possibly stop the truck before it reached Renni even if he wanted to.

Renni was gone, gone beyond hope of saving. All that would be left of the young life, all that would be left of George's hopes would be a bloody little mass, crushed and tattered. That and a great sorrow. Nothing more.

Through George's mind there whirled in a wild confusion, self-reproach because he had not taken better care of Renni, visions of the next few terrible seconds, foretastes of the sadness which the next few weeks would bring. He came near collapsing.

By this time the truck had roared over Renni, and on past, leaving behind a cloud of dust and bluish smoke.

Renni lay flat on the ground, not moving a limb. He was alive! He had not the slightest wound! He was only paralyzed by fright. That was why he dared not make a move. He had lain between the crushing wheels while sudden darkness, crashing and roaring, broke over him, passed in the twinkle of an eye and then vanished, leaving the bright friendly sunshine again.

When George rushed to him and found him safe and sound, picked him up and felt him all over, he could not believe that Renni had escaped whole from certain death, that nothing at all had happened to him.

Like a man possessed he pressed the puppy close, hugging the chubby warm body to him, stammering words of endearment mingled with threats and warnings. At last he came back to the garden with his clothes soiled, his hands dirty, but with an inexpressibly happy expression on his face. He closed the garden gate with a bang. Put down in the grass, Renni came to and performed a dance of joy around George. In his gaiety he ran over Kitty and sent her rolling. Kitty was ready enough to play with Renni, but she had to sneeze every time she came near him, for he smelled of street dust and burnt gasoline.

From that day on George redoubled the care with which he watched over Renni. He screwed a spring latch onto the garden gate so that it sprang shut whenever a delivery man or anyone else went in or out.

Renni was growing larger and larger. He could no longer be called a puppy, except as a pet name. He still had all the signs of puppyhood in his looks, his awkwardness and clumsiness, but he was no longer a pup. There was no way to tell whether he remembered the adventure in which he had almost lost his life. George declared that Renni was cured once and for all, that he would dodge any automobile and would be careful to keep off the highway. Mother Marie laughed. "Then why did you put the automatic lock on the garden gate?" she asked.

"To keep him from running around in the fields by himself," said George in self-defence.

The relations between master and dog became closer and more intimate from day to day. According to George, Renni realised that George owned him. As a matter of fact, Renni was firmly convinced that George was his personal property.

If George was gone for a few hours Renni might condescend to frolic with Kitty, who was always challenging him, but in a little while he would refuse to be tempted further and would lie waiting in front of the house door or peeping out the garden gate, with his big sharp ears pricked up. Those ears were very expressive. If he had to wait too long he would give vent to an impatient whine and then lapse into his silent waiting.

Once again longing would overcome him. He would lift his beautiful head and a soft, wailing howl would come from his rounded lips in long-drawn-out, high-pitched tones. They seemed to say, "Where is he? Why doesn't he come? Won't I ever see him again?" Renni's song of mourning voiced every imaginable complaint.

But he knew when George was coming, a long way off. Before he came into sight, before his steps could be heard by human ears, Renni's eager tail would be thumping the ground loudly, he would be getting up to greet his master with an outburst of joy. He would spring up on George as high as he could, try to kiss him, dash around like a whirlwind, come back to him again and again, and would not begin to calm down until he had been praised and petted extravagantly. As long as this dance of joy went on, nothing and nobody existed except George–not Kitty or Mother Marie, or a bite of his favourite food, or furniture or rugs or anything. He upset chairs, rolled over and over, pulled at a rug until it wrapped itself around his legs and threw him down. When he knocked dishes clattering around him they did not scare him or lessen his joyous madness in the least degree.

Later on Renni fell into the habit of getting hold of some piece of George's clothing–a cap, a shirt, a neckerchief; anything he could snatch up in a hurry he would take and stretch out on it just as though he had George safe forever, and now George could never leave him again. Anyone listening then could hear deep, soft, sighing breaths of joy and peace. As soon as George became aware of this habit he cut short the ceremony of greeting by throwing Renni something of his, and Renni was immediately satisfied.

Chapter III

ABOUT THIS TIME A SORT OF crisis arose between master and dog. Renni set his will against George's. Neither had the least suspicion what was going on. Olga was the cause of it all. Olga was a pretty, flashily dressed girl whom George met in one of the city parks and found very attractive.

From the very beginning Renni took a strong dislike to her. Gay, jolly, full of fun, apparently harmless, ready for everything, the girl set her cap for George. Naturally the dog had not the slightest idea of that, but in some instinctive way he felt her insincerity and simply could not stand her.

It happened this way. George had begun to take Renni with him when he went walking in the city. That was when Renni was about seven months old. "There's no need for him to have to wait for me," thought George. "I'll take him along and let him get used to me, let him learn to behave himself out in the world."

His mother suggested that George might learn something from it, too.

"Certainly," agreed George. He would always agree to anything reasonable. He had a great deal of sound sense and Mother Marie never said anything unreasonable. So they got along very nicely.

George led Renni by a leather leash, talked to him all the time and helped him out of the confusion and fear of the heavy traffic in the street. He took him on the street car, praised and petted him when Renni at first crept fearfully into a corner of the platform. "Now, now, that's right! That's your place! Good boy!

You're learning." People looked scornfully or smiled in friendly fashion according to the kind of people they were. George paid as little attention to them as Renni did to those who petted him. He kept his eye solely on his master.

When they reached open country George unsnapped the leash and turned the dog loose. Renni ran in wide joyful circles, galloping happily over the meadows, or rummaged about, his nose to the ground in obedience to some hunting impulse awake in him. If George called him he would stop instantly, dash up in wild career and act as overjoyed as though he had just discovered his master and was charmed to find him again after being away ever so long. Sometimes he would pay no heed to call or whistle, assume an air of independence, behave like a complete stranger. George put up with these whims, waited for them to end. He never thought of punishing the dog, but greeted him in all friendliness when he came up wagging his tail. Mother Marie was a good prophet when she said George too would learn from these trips together. George practised patience and came to know the dog better and better.

Most of the time Renni had his tongue out of his open mouth, sometimes because he was tired, sometimes because he was excited. He was often tired and often excited. He was panting nearly all the time.

Renni had several little adventures and encounters with strange dogs. On the street when he was on the short leash they seldom spoke to him, though George did not object to friendly meetings if they amounted only to the long ceremony of mutual sniffing. If a strange dog challenged to a fight, George would shorten the leash and say, "Come, Renni," and Renni would come at once. George took good care not to seem hostile toward the strange dog or try to drive him away. If he had it would only have excited Renni to attack and the battle would have been on. George wanted to keep Renni from becoming quarrelsome. If a stranger was especially stubborn, George had only to stoop down quickly and the troublemaker would scamper off as fast as he could for fear George would throw a stone at him.

When they came to a park George would sit down on a bench so Renni would have a chance to rest. Usually the dog would stretch out at his master's feet, yawn, pant a little and finally go to sleep. When he awakened no longer tired he overwhelmed George with demonstrations of affection. Often Renni set out quietly but wholeheartedly to climb George. He would stretch his forepaws up onto George's knee, and with great difficulty drag his hind legs up after them, and not be satisfied until he lay in George's lap. To be sure, he was three times too big for a lap dog. He covered George's lap completely and hung over in places. Not to mention that he got his long-suffering master's clothes into terrible shape.

Once it happened that a wire-haired fox terrier caught a whiff of Renni as he lay sleeping in the park, woke him up and challenged him. It was hard to tell whether it was a challenge to play or to fight. The fox terrier, not in the least embarrassed by George's presence, soon grew bold. He kept barking and even thrust his muzzle into Renni's flanks. Renni made no sound, just showed his teeth. The terrier was not to be bluffed. He was a brave little fellow and he snapped at Renni. Then George eased up on the leash. Renni shot to his feet and in a second the surprised little dog was wriggling between his paws. When Renni dropped him he fell to the ground and flew away as if bewitched. Renni at once lay down calmly at his master's feet. His expression seemed to say plainly enough, "That's that."

Several weeks passed before George and Renni went to the park again. This was the day Miss Olga put in an appearance. She came slowly along under the green shadows of the trees, very jaunty and assured. There were plenty of empty benches, but Olga picked out the one where George was sitting. Possibly the wide linden tree that shaded it influenced Olga in her choice; just possibly she had other motives. She took a seat, nodded–an uppish, scarcely perceptible nod–as if she wished to be left strictly alone.

Yet she was not really calm. She was forever picking and pulling at her clothes, at the sleeve of her blouse, at the wrinkles in her skirt, at her straw hat. Anyone observing her coolly could have seen how vain she was, and yet how unsure of herself. But George noticed nothing of the sort. He gazed at Olga attentively but by no means coolly. He liked her looks.

Renni had got up to sniff at Olga. She drove him away with an ill-natured gesture, and George put him in his place more sternly than usual. He lay down again as if it didn't matter.

"I'm sorry my dog . . ." stammered George.

Olga murmured, "Please don't mention it."

There the conversation lagged for a while. In a few moments she took a compact from her bag, unsnapped the tiny mirror, powdered her face and used her lipstick. Meanwhile her handbag fell to the ground. Of course it may have slipped down accidentally. Just possibly it had been given a little push. At any rate George hailed it as a bit of good fortune, picked it up quickly and started to hand it to its owner.

"Oh, thank you so much," said. Olga, now very friendly. "Perhaps you'll be kind enough to hold it till I get through. Otherwise you might have to pick it up again." Her laugh did not ring quite true. It sounded rehearsed. But it enchanted poor George. Only Renni seemed to catch its insincerity.

That was the beginning of the silent struggle between Olga and Renni. From then on George met Olga almost daily in the park. She was his first girl, and in his eyes could do no wrong. Olga knew from the start what she wanted, and she soon realized George's feeling about animals. If she did not share it, at least she was smart enough to make an honest effort to make Renni like her. It wasn't her fault that she failed. Once she tried to pet him. Renni avoided her hand. When she repeated the attempt, he raised his lips, showed his gleaming fangs and growled softly.

She had failed with Renni, but not with George. More and more he became her devoted slave. Such a state of affairs could not be kept long from Mother Marie. One day she asked him abruptly, "Have you got a girl?" Her eyes were laughing.

"Yes."

"I'm so glad," said Mother Marie. George threw his

arms around her neck, and then rushed out of the room.

It was not mentioned again by either of them until a night some weeks later when they were sitting up late talking. George sighed deeply.

"Renni's been acting queer here lately," he said.

"Queer?"

"He doesn't like Olga."

Now the whole story had to come out. Renni hadn't been cross, but he made his dislike quite evident.

"What do you think, Mother? Isn't that hard to understand?"

She smiled in a peculiar way.

"I do not find it the least hard to understand, my dear boy. You'll simply have to find another girl."

"Another girl! There isn't any other."

"Don't be foolish."

"On Renni's account?"

"Certainly."

"Why? Because he happens to be jealous?"

"Nonsense. Renni isn't jealous. He just happens to be right, you know. That's the reason."

"Why, Mother, do you really, seriously want me to do what Renni thinks best? Give up a splendid girl like that for the sake of a dog?"

"You're in love. You couldn't possibly be unprejudiced."

"Do you actually think Renni has better judgment than I have?"

"No. But his intuition, his instinct, is sure."

"Now, see here, Mother. I was guided by my own instinct. Otherwise, I'd hardly have fallen in love."

"That's where you're wrong, son. A mere attraction made up your mind for you. But let's not try to settle it by arguing. We'd never get anywhere that way. I'll tell you what to do. Bring Miss Olga to see me."

"Oh, Mother, that's what I meant to do anyway. Thank you so much."

"Don't thank me. All I want is to meet her."

"All right. That's settled. I'll ask only one thing of you. Don't be prejudiced against Olga."

His mother interrupted him, laughing.

"Which side do you really think I'm on, son–the dog's or yours?"

George fell silent. He was a bit ashamed.

The very next day he brought Olga home with him. As usual Renni paid no attention to her, and his greeting to his master was much shorter and less cordial than usual. Then he went and lay down in his usual place.

Olga came in radiant, perfectly certain she would carry all before her. She looked everything over with bright eyes that missed nothing. She felt very near her goal. In the sitting-room Mother Marie bade her welcome with utmost friendliness. Again her sharp eyes made a swift but searching survey of the room, and again she liked all she saw. She thought it would be an easy thing to win the mother over.

But it wasn't easy at all. The two women were too opposite in their natures. Even George soon began to feel the great contrast between his mother's frankness and Olga's artificiality. Beside his mother's clear, sweet face, Olga's painted features were almost painful to him. And her words made him feel that they too were, so to speak, painted. When he heard his mother talk so naturally and with such a sincere ring in her voice, he was uncomfortable. He wriggled in his chair and soon stopped talking. The conversation limped again and again.

Gradually Olga lost her assurance. This may have been why she did not try to control herself when Kitty appeared, but gave a little shriek of disgust.

"Phew! A cat!"

Mother Marie hugged the little thing and asked innocently, "Don't you like our Kitty?"

"No," confessed Olga quickly and without considering. "I do not like cats. They're all treacherous."

At that moment George knew he was done with Olga. Renni growled softly. Olga realised her mistake, but she was past caring now, so she let herself go.

"I can't understand at all," she said in the tone of a schoolteacher, "how anybody could stand having one of these spiteful creatures in the house. I never will understand it."

It was the only sincere thing Olga had said, but it was a declaration of war on Mother Marie.

Smiling and conciliatory, she answered, "There are many people who think just as you do, Miss Olga. I know that well enough. But nothing can be done for us others. We're just that foolish."

George took Olga home in a taxi. As soon as she was alone with him, she regained all her self-confidence. She counted on her hold over him. This young man was her private property, she thought. Oh, she was certain of success. Now she'd triumph over that old woman.

"Darling," she whispered, "when we're married, your mother will live somewhere else, of course. You know, sweetheart, a mother-in-law in the house–it never works."

She kissed him. "You surely won't expect that of me. You know I could never stand it, though I'd stand almost anything for you."

She realised she had lost when George loosened her arms and said earnestly, "I shall never be separated from my mother."

But even then she would not give up.

"Is that so? Then you'll have to be separated from me."

He said nothing.

Her tearful reproach, "You don't love me," fell flat because anger dried her tears and because he had a ready answer.

"After what you have just asked, I think it's you who don't love me."

It did not take them long to part. Olga was spiteful, George sad.

Olga comforted herself. She thought, "He'll come back all right. He'll have to swallow his words. This can't possibly be the end. I know he won't hold out against me."

But George did hold out. Going home that evening, he felt deeply hurt. His mother said nothing. She saw what had happened and did not need to speak of it. George, too, had nothing to say.

Again George began to take long walks with the dog, lonely wanderings in the open fields.

After a few days a letter came. Mother Marie handed it over to her son. He opened it, glanced at it, hastily crumpled it up and threw it into the waste basket.

"From Olga," he said wearily.

Nothing more was said. It was the last time they mentioned her name. Mother Marie stroked the dog with a special tenderness. She had known all the time that Renni would win.

Chapter IV

SOME WAY FROM HOME, IN THE midst of the stubble fields, George made the acquaintance of a man. Really it was Renni who struck up a friendship with the man's police dog, about his own age. The two dogs greeted each other with an unusual cordiality and immediately began to play. They tore about, gaily chasing each other, describing great circles, whirling unexpectedly, and rolling over and over.

"Pasha!" cried the stranger, and when Pasha failed to

obey immediately, he roared out in an angry, threatening tone, "Pasha, to heel!"

The dog was visibly frightened. He came toward his master at a dead run, then stopped and crawled on his belly as though he were humbly begging forgiveness.

"Call in your dog, why don't you?" the stranger bellowed to George.

"Oh, no," he answered. "Renni may run all he wants to." And in some astonishment he asked the stranger, "You don't carry a whip, do you?"

"Why, of course I do."

"But of course you wouldn't strike him."

"When he deserves punishment, punishment is what he gets."

George was horrified.

"Haven't you any sympathy for the poor beast?"

"Sentimental twaddle!" growled the stranger.

He was perhaps forty years old, very slender, very tall, with a military bearing. His face was somewhat secretive, and George thought he could detect a strain of hardness in it. Still there was a weak look in his eyes too. George could not quite make up his mind what to think of him.

"And you?" asked the stranger. "How do you punish your hound?"

"I don't."

The stranger reproved him, shaking his head. "Punishment is necessary for man and beast."

"Perhaps," admitted George. "Perhaps. But I've never whipped my dog and I never intend to."

"You're a queer bird," laughed the stranger.

"Would you favour whipping people too by way of punishment?" inquired George.

"Well, it wouldn't hurt any."

"And children?"

"With children it's absolutely necessary, just as it is with dogs."

"You mean that dogs are like children–children who can't talk?"

"With dogs or with children you can get quickest results by slapping them, or, if need be, by thrashing them."

"The results will be quick, all right, but I'm not so sure they'll be good," said George.

Renni came running. He leaped up on his master, wagging his tail joyfully, and George gave him a friendly welcome.

"You ought never to permit such liberties."

"Not permit them?" George bridled at the censure in his tone and went on petting Renni, who whirled around him, tail wagging madly. "These liberties as you call them are the finest thing I know. I want my dog to be as free with me as I am with him."

The stranger did not deign to answer. He studied Renni and with a rough jerk put Pasha up beside him. They were as like as two peas.

"Have you got your dog's pedigree?" he asked George, and when the latter admitted, "No, not yet," he went on:

"When you pay good money for a dog, you must always get his pedigree. Here's Pasha's."

He pulled papers from his pocket and handed them to George. It developed that Pasha and Renni were brothers. George read the long, long list of Renni's ancestors with something like reverence. There was many a champion among them who had won blue ribbons. When he handed the papers back, the stranger introduced himself as Karl Stefanus. His grandparents had moved from the north and settled in this country.

After this George and Karl met often and took long walks with their dogs. The dogs always got along better than the masters, who constantly argued over the question–to whip or not to whip. "I wish you'd humour me by not striking Pasha when I'm around."

"Of course I can't promise that."

"Then I've had enough."

"You're an odd piece," grumbled Karl, but he didn't strike Pasha.

He thought George mildly and harmlessly insane. In time he came to have a certain sympathy for this man, who was so sincere and genuine and whom he accused of being wishy-washy and sentimental when he was neither. The only reason George kept up the acquaintance was on Pasha's account. Sometimes Karl would call his dog in a harsh commanding voice. Pasha obeyed instantly and seemed, as he crept up on his belly, to be repenting for something wrong he hadn't done.

"Now you ought to praise him," said George.

"Wouldn't think of it. Only spoil him." But still he gave him a gruff "Good boy!"

Then George called Renni and up he came rushing like a gust of wind, waving his tail, leaping beside himself for joy. George patted him.

"See?" he said triumphantly. "See how much better this is?"

The other did not answer. But the next time he wanted to know whether Renni was to be trained for anything useful. "What you need is a toy dog, a lap dog."

When George looked at him questioningly, he added, "A police dog like that needs some useful occupation. If he doesn't get it, he'll degenerate."

Meanwhile Renni and Pasha carried on a lot of conversation, canine fashion. Of course they didn't use human words, but their way of talking worked perfectly for them.

Renni would scratch eagerly at a mole hill. Naturally

he wouldn't get results. He'd ask Pasha, "Give me a little help here."

And immediately Pasha would answer, "He won't let me."

Renni would chase a mouse and call out to Pasha, "Catch it!"

Pasha would give the same answer: "He won't let me."

"Can't you have any fun at all?" Renni asked, wondering.

Pasha would say sadly, "No. Practically everything is forbidden. I don't know yet just what I *am* allowed to do and so I'm very careful."

"Why?"

"Well, I'm afraid."

Renni asked curiously, "Afraid of what?"

"Why, you know! Of the pain."

Renni was amazed. "I don't know. What's pain?"

"It's something that comes from Him," Pasha said. "Hasn't your master ever caused you any pain?"

"No, never."

"But surely you know that long slithering thing that

whistles so when He brings it down on us–the thing that cuts so, clear to the bone?"

Renni shook his head. He didn't know what Pasha was talking about. It didn't make sense to him. He suggested this must be the reason why Pasha was unhappy.

"How can anyone be happy?" Pasha's eye was sad. "Oh, to be sure, right at first, when I didn't know about such things, I was happy. But the first time it happened my happiness was over. At the first blow I lost control of my feelings, I was so afraid. When the blows kept coming one after another, striking me down again and again, I was scared for good and all. You can't imagine how horribly that thing hurts. It burns you through and through. It sets your blood on fire. When it reaches the worst, I simply lose all hope, all courage. That's what makes me so sad."

"Oh," cried Renni, "I would have bitten."

"I did try it . . . but the way the blows rained down . . . it was enough to kill me. . . ."

"You ought to have run away."

"Don't say that! Run away from Him? Impossible! I love Him. In spite of it all I love Him more than anything else."

After this Renni timidly kept to George's side when they went into Karl's room for a visit. Pasha, at an order, crept at once to his place and did not dare make the slightest move. It was a modest room, sparingly furnished with hard chairs, a hard sofa, a bare table, cheap bric-a-brac. Karl offered George a little refreshment.

"Have you made your mind up yet what your Renni is to be?"

"Not yet," George admitted uncertainly, stroking Renni, who had pricked up his ears at mention of his name.

"I'm going to train Pasha for police work."

"How do you go about it?"

"Well, the fundamental thing, absolute obedience, he already has. The other points I shall soon teach him. Here–" he interrupted himself–"take this book. You'll find directions in it for all types of training–police work, messenger work, Red Cross service, and Seeing

Eyes for the blind. You'll soon get the idea how it's done."

"Interesting!" George reached for the book. "I'm really very much obliged to you."

Renni was looking Karl steadily in the face as though he understood every word.

"Of course you have to wait until the dog is full grown before you begin the training seriously."

"Oh, of course," agreed George. And Renni seemed, to judge from his expression, to be entirely of that opinion.

As they started to go, Karl smiled. "That book will cure you of your soft-hearted nonsense."

When he saw that George was about to give it back, he laughed aloud. "Don't worry. You won't have to train yourself to torture animals. Why, even I am not really cruel."

Pasha might have had something to say on that score if he'd been able to talk in human fashion.

When George reached the street, he drew a long breath. Renni, feeling suddenly free, almost went crazy with joy. At home George showed the book to his mother. When she said, "Let me have it," he did so readily enough, merely asking, "Why?"

Her answer was a brief "Just so."

That, to be sure, was not a very clear reason, but it served between this understanding pair. Mother Marie held the book out to Renni. "Look at this. It's meant for you."

The dog sniffed at it for a second and drew back as if afraid.

"Maybe he guesses what's in it." She laughed.

After a few days she laid the book down before George.

"Well?" he asked.

"Read it yourself." This time she did not smile.

George repeated the question urgently. "I'd like to know what you think, Mother."

Mother Marie went out of the room without a word. George believed that he had her opinion. So he read it himself, but he was not, as Karl had prophesied, convinced by what he read, not by any means. Moreover, the soft-hearted nonsense remained uncured. Instead, it went wild. George became all excited. His gentle manner utterly vanished whenever he thought or spoke of what he had read.

"What do you say, Mother?" he said, half-angry and half-worried. "'Every once in a while a switching! Every once in a while a sound thrashing!' What do you say to that?"

"Everyone according to his own judgment," said Mother Marie, trying to calm him. "There's no denying the wonderful things dogs have accomplished."

George hastened to defend his position. "They would have done just as much if not more without punishment. A policeman told me once that while dogs were in training they were not allowed to be struck in any circumstances."

Mother Marie smiled. "That might be so."

"Of course it's so. I saw the man working with his dog. The reason I spoke to him was because I liked the way he went about it and from then on my desire to own a dog like his became stronger and stronger." He tapped the book. "Here they warn you not to attribute a soul to animals, or a real capacity to think. They settle everything with the word instinct. *Instinct!* Could there possibly be a word more meaningless than instinct? Oh, how arrogant men are! They think that they can settle the whole inner life of creatures as simply as that. These wonderful dogs are mysterious because they seek our company! They are made servile only by our craving to command! Just because they help us, because they want to help us!

"We are a long, long way from valuing properly their unbounded love, their unquestioning yet intelligent devotion. We take it altogether too much for granted. We can't appreciate their simple, candid natures, their inability to lie, because we don't always tell the truth ourselves. Who was it said, 'The more I see of men, the better I like dogs'?"

George, ordinarily so quiet, had suddenly become an orator and a high-flying orator at that. His mother listened to him in astonishment. "Now, you're going too far."

"I couldn't possibly go too far." His excitement

swept him along. "Too far? Impossible! What have men ever done to repay all the loyalty, all the sacrifices, all the countless proofs of idolatry they have always taken as a matter of course? Feed them? Ridiculous! The dog was originally a beast of prey. He could very well have provided for his own food. To be sure, he might have become extinct if he hadn't come to man of his own free will thousands of years ago. But it was a pretty poor piece of business for him when he did, though a very profitable one for man. Just think of all the irresistible ways they have of attaching themselves to us.

"They don't harm chickens, geese or other animals that belong to men. They guard and protect them. That's been going on for thousands of years. You know how it is in hunting. The dog lays the game down at his master's feet, no matter how great his temptation may be. That's been impressed on him through countless generations, and no one takes the trouble to wonder at it for a second. Dogs serve and men command–and some men whip. Just like that! No one stops to think what a mountain peak of debt man owes to dogs. Perhaps in America they are more humane. I hear that hydrophobia is not so common over there."

At this moment Renni came slowly up, looked at his master questioningly and acted a bit timid. George's violent words had puzzled the dog, for ordinarily he spoke in soft tones. George bent down, relaxed, laughed.

"Well, what do you want, old fellow?"

The dog immediately began a swift and joyous wagging of his tail, leaped up on George, laid his forepaws on his breast. "No," whispered George. "No. I'll never beat you. Never." He caught the beautiful head in both hands, fondled his forehead at the point where, over the eyes, a slight furrow divided his skull and the silky hair felt even silkier. When he released him, Renni started tearing around and around the room, and cutting all kinds of capers. George's laugh encouraged him. Mother Marie was saying, "Well, is Renni to go on without learning anything useful? That would be too bad."

"What do you mean, without learning anything useful?"

"Didn't you just now promise you'd never strike him? And if there's no training without punishment . . ."

"Training, Mother? If that's training, I don't think much of it."

"Perhaps you're right. It's only a word. Maybe Karl likes the book because it expresses his own ideas. Maybe other books favour different methods, like your policeman friend. Anyhow, we have plenty of time, haven't we, Renni?"

At his name the dog, who had been scuffling with Kitty and was now standing directly over her, pricked up his ears. The cat seized the chance, slipped neatly between his legs and in the twinkling of an eye seated herself on Mother Marie's lap, purring loudly.

Chapter V

ONE DAY GEORGE TOOK RENNI TO the man from whom he had got him as a puppy. A friendly old housekeeper showed George in and patted Renni, who wagged his tail gently but acted a bit shy.

"Fine fellow," she praised. "One of ours?"

George said he was.

"Just come in," she urged him. "The master will be pleasantly surprised."

A violent uproar sounded from within. "Mr. Vogg

is just having a little understanding with his boy," the housekeeper explained.

When they entered his room, Vogg ignored them and went on swearing at the kennel boy who stood crushed before him.

"You lazy rascal!" he cried. "You dyed-in-the-wool loafer! I'll skin you alive!"

While he went on roaring, George looked around the room. The furniture was old-fashioned. On the wall hung many photographs of proud white horses, sharp fox terriers, sturdy police dogs. The room had such an unmistakable air of comfort and content that George, in spite of the man's yelling, felt himself at peace. Finally the kennel boy got away. Vogg turned to George and asked quite calmly, "Something I can do for you?"

George said very politely, "I'd just like to know whether you're pleased with Renni."

From the yard, evidently from the kennels, there came up a subdued but vigorous barking. Renni, his nose pointed straight down and his ears straight up, listened attentively toward the floor, but he did not even move when the man's hand seized his coat rather roughly and pressed on his hind quarters trying in vain to push him down.

"It's he all right," said Vogg. He took the dog by the head, lifted up his lips, opened his mouth and then turned him loose. "In good shape," he murmured. Now Renni sniffed at the man carefully, wagged his tail first slowly then a bit faster, rubbed his neck against Vogg's trousers, and finally lay down quietly. His head leaned more and more sharply forward at each outburst of barking from below. The two men looked at this byplay in silence.

"Properly handled in every way," Vogg said. A glance at George went with the sharp question, "Not too much whipping?"

"No whipping at all," smiled George. "I couldn't strike a dog." He felt a little uneasy and did not regain his composure until Vogg cried, "Good for you! That's exactly my own idea.

"Of the people who beat dogs, some use a whip," he went on, "or even a stick, because it's the most convenient and least troublesome way for them to come to terms. Perhaps they have a scrap of feeling for the animal. Others whip because it's the easiest way to prove they're masters of something. They are almost always browbeaten themselves by their bosses or their wives. When they start beating a dog, they're simply getting even, relieving their humiliated feelings. They don't think of the torture they're giving the poor creature in their care. Worst of all are those who keep a dog only to give free rein to their cruel impulses. When they start beating him they actually enjoy it and that makes them keep on beating him. Curse their hides!"

George was charmed to hear, from this expert, views so much like his own. "Do you think it possible to get results in training without whipping?"

After a short, grim laugh came the answer: "The man would have to be remarkably patient and the dog wonderfully gifted." Renni's head was lying on George's knee. He stroked it tenderly. Vogg continued as if he were thinking aloud, "Without whipping? . . . Nowadays, trainers who make lions or tigers jump through burning hoops or do some other stupid thing, why, these fellows actually assert they've accomplished it without punishment. I don't believe it." He was almost shouting now. "I can't, and don't, and won't believe it!" Again he gave a short, angry laugh. "It's a lie, of course. Why should lions and tigers squat on silly pedestals, or ride on trembling horses, or do all those other fool things out of sheer good nature? You can tell just by looking at them how scared they are, how their spirit has been crushed out of them. Without whipping, without the iron bar, the rhinoceros whip and all the other tortures! Blazes! It's absurd!

"The public swallow such confounded crazy lies because they want to enjoy a thrill without having their consciences hurt them. Writers tell the dear people that a tiger can be happy only in prison. And the dear people believe what they're told. All you need do is say something firmly enough and keep on saying it, and people will believe it no matter how absurd it is, how impossible. The legend that wild beasts from India and Africa long for the cage and the circus is far from the worst lie that's being swallowed hook, line and sinker. Merciful God! They're crowding far more horrible things than that into the empty heads and the calloused hearts of men. The poison is spreading like a contagion. Like a plague. Just because it's dinned into them, people here in Europe accept the crushing idea that *men themselves* prefer slavery to freedom! . . . Well, let's not talk about it."

He stopped and sat brooding, staring straight ahead. George was afraid to disturb him. Finally the man lifted his eyes again. "What was it I really wanted to say?"

George said in a low tone, "I don't know."

Vogg said, "I'm sorry. I get off the track when I'm talking with someone who treats dogs properly. . . . Well, come here to me, Renni."

The dog walked over to him at once. "You have a good master." Renni wagged his tail and arched his body in pure friendliness.

Chapter VI

FOR DAYS AT A TIME RAIN HAD BEEN pouring from the grey heavens. The water splashed incessantly on the roof, in the garden, in the street. The rain kept on obstinately without a pause, drumming loud at nights on the window-panes, and the air had turned icy cold.

Renni was let out for a run only now and then. He lay in front of the fireplace watching the flames contentedly with Kitty crowding close to his breast. She too watched the play of the flames with a deep show of interest. Renni, overcome by drowsiness, would blink and try to bed his head on his forepaws, but every time he tried it the cat would slap him warningly in the face. Renni would quiver, wake up obediently, hold up his head for a while until he got too drowsy again; then his head would sink slowly and he would get another warning. Finally he threw himself over on his side, and Kitty cuddled up against his neck. Now he could sleep.

Once his master's voice awakened him. George stood at the window and asked his mother, " Do you see what I see?"

Mother Marie looked fixedly at the garden gate. "It looks like a bundle of rags washed down by the rain."

"No," said George. "That rag bag moved just now. There it goes again. It's alive." He hastened to the entryway and rushed out. Lying close against the garden gate was an old, slick-haired pointer in a terrible state, completely exhausted, covered from head to foot with mud. He was dripping with rain and shivering. He shrank back in terror when the gate opened and drew into himself when George came near him. He tried to dodge, but he was too weak. He crouched down flat against the soaking wet ground and looked up fearfully and pitifully as only a dying animal can.

"You poor chap," said George softly. "Come on in."

But the dog did not dare risk a movement. "Come! Come on!" George begged him in gentlest tones. He was shocked. Still the dog did not move. George stooped down, petted the wet skin, felt the horrible thinness, and went on talking in a kind voice.

"Come on, I want to help you. You're hungry and cold. Trust me. Come on! Come on!"

The dog looked up at George's smiling face, doubting, amazed; he hesitated but finally began to understand that nothing threatened him. Still George had to push him over the threshold into the garden, had to encourage him with words and sometimes help him with his hands until at last he got the pointer to follow him, on crouching legs. In the entryway George rubbed him partially dry. It took a good many old rags and pieces of sacking.

"Wait," said Mother Marie. "I think there's some

milk and rice left. The poor thing's almost starved to death. Let's see whether he can eat anything at all, and if he eats it whether he can keep it down." She too was deeply moved.

At first the dog did not even dare to come up to the dish. Mother and son coaxed him. Finally he made up his mind, screwed up his courage and in the twinkling of an eye swallowed the few bites of soft rice that were allowed him.

"That's enough for the moment," warned Mother Marie. "Give him a swallow of warm milk. Not much. Just a little."

George held the pointer's muzzle shut, lifted his lips at one side so they made a kind of funnel and poured a teaspoonful of the milk down his throat. Then another and another. The dog accepted them as he had everything else, without will of his own. He seemed empty of life, almost unconscious.

"Now a bed for him and a warm cover," said George.

Then they carried him to the kitchen stove from which the heat was still pouring, wrapped him up in an old quilt and laid him down carefully. The trembling had ceased. He went to sleep under their hands, the deep sleep of utter exhaustion.

Meanwhile Renni had been snuffling and blowing with loud puffs outside the kitchen door. "In the morning, old boy, in the morning," George comforted him. Renni knew there was a strange dog in the house and it was a long time before he quieted down.

Even the next day Renni did not get to see the pointer for some little while. Only the kitten slipped into the room where they were washing the creature. There she sat on the little window sill, daintily washing her face. Once she'd seen the old pointer, her curiosity was satisfied. He stood unresisting, without any will of his own, in the warm water of the wooden tub, while the cleansing waves poured over him. Twice, three times mother and son filled the tub with fresh warm water, and every time the tub had to be washed out. They took great pains. When at length they let the hunter go, they helped him out of the tub and watched him shake himself, not very vigorously, for he did not have strength enough for that. Still, a fine spray of drops showered around his pitiful figure.

"He must have been handsome once on a time," George said, while Mother Marie busied herself rubbing the pointer dry. Big, brown spots appeared on his coat. His breast was snow-white, and his head brown with a narrow white stripe running from his nose up to his forehead. His dark brown ears hung low. They were so long they could be pulled together over his nose. There were scattering brown marks on his legs.

"He's going to be handsome again soon," promised the mother, "if we can feed him up well."

"What'll we call him?" asked George.

They tried ever so many names but the pointer answered to none of them.

"Let's call him Nemo," suggested George, who knew a little Latin. "He really isn't anybody. Just a shipwrecked life, a lost soul."

Nemo had quickly swallowed a second portion of milk and rice. Then they brought him out into the hall. He still crept along with his legs bent and his tail close between his legs. So he met Renni. And at first he appeared terror-stricken. Renni was interested. Nemo threw himself on his back and stretched his four legs out–a gesture which meant, "Please don't hurt me." Renni had not the slightest idea of hurting the pitiful guest. He wagged his tail affectionately, sniffing Nemo all over. Kitty came up and thrust an experimental paw at the stranger. He was puzzled by the cat, puzzled by Renni's friendliness. Very, very slowly he gathered himself together and risked a shy kiss in Renni's direction. But he only reached one eye. Renni did not mind. On the contrary, he set in to wash the poor thin face thoroughly with his tongue.

"Well," smiled Mother Marie, "they're going to make friends."

"Renni likes to get along well with everybody," declared George. "He realises that Nemo is out of luck."

"Kitty seems to feel that too," Mother Marie pointed out. There were three now bedded down together on Renni's mattress.

Nemo went to sleep again at once. Kitty crawled

up, purred a while, and then fell asleep. Renni acted as though he were going to keep watch over them but in a few minutes he too drowsed off. In the middle of the night Nemo waked, stretched and sighed. Renni immediately was wide awake. That went along with his ability to fall asleep instantly, a gift he shared with all dogs. Kitty didn't move. It was pitch dark in the house.

"Why are you so sad?" asked Renni.

"I want my master," whispered Nemo.

"You ought to have stayed with Him."

"How can I stay with Him when He drives me away?"

"If He drove you away, why do you want Him?"

"But . . . I love Him . . . in spite . . ."

"Why would He drive you away?"

"Well, because I'm old, because I'm no longer good for anything. Oh, the last few days were terrible. Blows, nothing to eat, kicks."

"I don't know anything about such things."

"Why, I always got whipped. A long time ago He

whipped me whenever I couldn't resist running after a rabbit. Of course, that was forbidden."

"You oughtn't to have done it."

"I got over the habit, but how much pain it caused me! Or perhaps I could not find a partridge that He'd shot. A whipping for me! Maybe He'd really missed it. Still . . . a whipping."

"And you love Him, you dumb dog?"

"No, I'm not dumb. Not at all. Oh, but He was nice to me, too. It was wonderful to be petted by Him when He was happy. I can never forget it. . . . Alas, He wasn't happy very often."

"And can you forget how He drove you away?"

"No, that was too awful."

"How did it happen?"

"He kicked me out of the house. In spite of the pain in my body I scratched at His door. He whipped me away. Again and again. I felt as if I were going to die."

Kitty's fine voice said, "I can't understand you people. Things like that could happen to me only once, and a mighty short once, too. I'd scratch. I'd scratch until He bled, and then I'd run away." Now with her back arched and her fur bristling with sparks she looked savage indeed. The dogs stared at her.

"Don't you love your master then?" stammered Renni.

"Nobody's my master," declared Kitty. "To obey anyone who likes to whip–only you silly dogs are capable of that."

"I don't know you when you're like this," said Renni in a humble tone.

"Well then, you know me now." Kitty quieted down, rolled up gently against Renni's side and purred. For a while they were all silent.

"What a kind master you have!" whispered Nemo. "I envy you. It's great to have a thing like this happen to me at the end of my life. I'd never have thought there was so much kindness anywhere, so much pity. I haven't any way to tell you how much good the help I've received here has done me. I was on my last legs after wandering about for days in this awful weather, after the loneliness, the hunger. It took all my strength.

I'd like to love your master . . . but I don't know. Love for my old master, cruel as He was to me, is still firm in my heart. I can't root it out. Do you hear me?"

But nether Kitty nor Renni heard the poor pointer's whispering. They were asleep. For a long time Nemo looked sadly into the dark. Finally slumber wrapped him too. Uneasy dreams brought back vague images of the suffering he had endured. His legs pressed close against his body, twitching violently as though he were running. He whimpered in a high, choking voice which did not reach very far. Much later he slipped into the depths of unconscious sleep, and that gave him strength again.

There is a barrier between man and beast; even when they live together on the best of terms, distance lies between them. Those two good people, George and his mother, had not the slightest inkling of the night-time conversation of their protégés. They were happy to see the friendship which Renni, Kitty and Nemo had formed. They were happy when the three ate their meals together from the same dish, and when Renni and Kitty drew back to leave most of it to Nemo, who devoured all that was left in gluttonous eagerness.

"Renni acts like a gentleman," George praised his dog.

"And Kitty is a perfect lady," smiled Mother Marie.

"Look, won't you, Mother? Nemo's already getting a little stronger."

He called the pointer, who at once crept humbly up, lay down and rolled over on his back at George's feet, wagging his tail timidly. George petted him, talked kindly to him.

"Now, Nemo, don't you be afraid. Don't act so queer," he said.

It did not help. The old dog was hearing a strange name instead of the one he was used to. He had found a place of safety here, but he did not feel at home. His thoughts were elsewhere. At every second he expected some new abuse, and he could not believe in this continuing kindness. There was something uncanny about it. It disturbed him. Renni watched while Nemo was petted, without the slightest jealousy. Kitty often challenged Nemo to play, but Nemo could not play. Real freedom prevailed only when the three animals were left alone. George and his mother accepted the shy nature of the pointer, and gave up trying to change him or make a closer friendship with him.

Chapter VII

LIFE GLIDED ALONG IN THE SAME OLD peaceful way.

"I'm anxious to try an experiment, to see whether kindness can accomplish all that we hope. Or more. You see, Mother, don't you, how clever and willing Renni is? If it can be done, fine! If not, well, I'll just let it go."

"What are you going to make of him?"

"I don't want him to become cruel, a man-hunter, leaping at the throats of criminals. That wouldn't be the sort of job I'd like myself. Renni must be helpful. Do good. That's what he's fitted for by nature."

Now an interesting time began, for, very quietly George started to try Renni out in methodical training. To his delight he found remarkable talents in the dog, gifts which were quite obviously awakened by kindness, and increased more and more by praise. Again and again George caught a certain look in Renni's eyes. A look of unlimited confidence, of utter devotion, and not only eagerness to understand, but joyful understanding itself. Moreover, there was a mute, insistent questioning, as though Renni encouraged George to give him some sort of command, which he would be eager to obey.

It took very little to induce Renni to lie still when George walked away, perfectly still instead of jumping up and running after him. That was the first lesson. George would say, "Lie down, old man," and Renni, at the fifth or sixth trial, grasped what was wanted of him. He would drop as though struck by lightning at the first word of the command. He was praised and petted without stint. George talked to him often and long, and

Renni would listen with ears pricked up, nose pointed down.

"We're going to do something really worth while, we two," said George. "We'll show Karl all right what can be done without the whip. Perhaps then he'll treat poor Pasha better, eh?"

Renni acted as though he understood every word. The only thing he lacked was speech. The only thing, thought George, and every time he felt himself strangely moved by the word "only." How close a dog can get to a man, and still how far, how very far we stay from each other, in spite of our friendship and devotion.

It was a long time before Renni reached the point where he understood George's outstretched hand as a sign for him to lie down. It was a long time before he would let George go away, would stay quietly in his place and only hurry after him when George raised his arm or called. Many a time during this period of training vexation welled up in George's heart and he was near scolding, but he always took a few deep breaths and recalled his thoughts about the helpless fellow. And then he remembered, "Why, we've started Renni out a good deal younger than is usually recommended. I mustn't forget that, must I, old man?" Sometimes he would stand in front of Renni and say softly to him, "How could anyone mistreat you, brother of mine?" So, ordinarily, good nature took the place of vexation. Yet, alone with the dog, George had a pretty tough time of it. He kept their difficulties from his mother. They took the most serious pains. They went out in the afternoons a long way from town, a long way from home, and if Renni had anything to do with it, a long way from Karl. Renni didn't like to have Karl around one little bit, and felt he could get along nicely without Pasha.

Meanwhile Nemo sunned himself on the gravel paths of the garden, accepting the kitten's coquetry indifferently and the mother's kindness with great humility. He rested as only a weary, broken exile rests after a life painful and burdensome.

George and Renni did not work with any degree of regularity. There were days when George did not feel like it, gave it up and let his thoughts wander elsewhere–to memories of Olga, the wish for a new friend, man or woman, or the little everyday worries of his life.

And then at times it was Renni who did not seem interested. He would apparently have forgotten all he had learned and be unable to learn anything new. The two would walk along mechanically side by side. Sometimes Renni would run ahead and swing about in wide circles; then at the least call he would come back to George's left side. For in all circumstances and no matter what his humour, he was always obedient.

But after they met Bettina they took a fresh interest in life. That occurred one day when Renni was lying perfectly still on the ground as he had been ordered, and George had gone off some distance. He was just on the point of raising his hand to call the dog to him, when he saw a girl stop beside the dog, bend over, and start talking to him. George walked slowly up and heard her say, "Fine fellow! Good pup! And you're handsome, too.

I'd like to pet you, you dear, but I don't quite dare."

Renni lay still, blinking at the girl without even raising his head, and only permitted himself the slightest wag of his tail.

"Please go on and pet him," George smiled. "He won't bite."

The girl raised startled eyes. "Oh, I beg your pardon. I saw the dog lying there, and . . ." she broke off in confusion.

George gave the sign which released Renni from his motionless waiting. He sprang to his feet and joyfully whirled around his master, and with the same exuberance around the new acquaintance, and she petted him to her heart's content.

George looked at the girl with interest. She was not pretty, but young and sweet. She was very simply dressed, without a hat. Her heavy russet hair was wound about her head in thick braids.

"Why does the–" she interrupted herself. "What is the beautiful thing's name?" And when she learned his name she resumed, "Why must he lie there all by himself?"

"It's an experiment. I'm getting ready to train him for war service."

"Oh dear! The poor thing's in for a lot of whipping." She petted Renni, who looked up at her almost laughing. "Renni, good boy," she went on; "you poor, good dog!"

George would have liked to ask, "Do I look cruel?" but what he said was, "Does he look to you like a whipped dog?"

She shrugged her shoulders. "No, not at all. But dogs are so goodhearted and forgiving–how can you tell?"

"Well, you'll just have to take my word for it, Miss. This Renni of mine has never yet had a blow, not a single one in his whole life."

"Really?" she cried. "I declare. That's wonderful." She knelt down and held Renni's head against her breast. "Do you really have such a good master?"

"You see, Miss, I'm trying an experiment in training the dog. I want to accomplish without punishment what others can only do with the whip or the stick."

She beamed. "Oh, you'll do it. I know you will. The dog is so smart, so willing and so gifted. . . . Please don't call me 'Miss,'" she said with a gesture of sincerity. Her small face turned a dark red. "My name is Bettina Holman. My friends call me Bettina."

She felt at ease with this young man. He gave her his name in return and insisted she call him George. Bettina told him her father had been a railroad man and was now on a pension. She had no mother. Her three grown brothers were employed as electricians or machinists. She herself, the youngest, was starting out to find a place as a servant girl. "It's very hard," she said, sighing. Being only eighteen, she had never worked.

While she petted Renni she listened to what George told her of himself, of his mother, of the dog fancier, Vogg; she heard his theories about animals in general and dogs in particular.

When they separated, they were already friends. George went home in a state of suppressed excitement. For the present he said nothing to his mother of this meeting, nor anything about his experiment with Renni.

The next day he met Bettina by appointment at the same place. From then on they met regularly at various places in the open country.

"What I want Renni to do is to learn to hunt for wounded men. He must find his man; then run quickly back to his master; then lead him to the spot. It's a hard, an awfully hard job."

Bettina was full of confidence. "Hard? Maybe–but Renni will get it all right, won't you, Renni? It won't take you long."

"Well, it won't be as simple as all that, Bettina. It calls for practice, pains, patience. Any amount of patience."

"You have patience." The girl smiled without coquetry. "See how kind you are with me."

"What do you mean? As if I needed patience with you! You're a dear."

She changed the subject. "We'll need help–someone to play wounded."

George caught her hand. "Thank you, Bettina."

She withdrew her hand which he let go reluctantly. "Thank me? Why?"

"Well, because you said 'we.'"

She blushed a little, hesitated. "Perhaps my brothers . . ."

When George came home in high spirits, his mother said, "A girl . . . ? Don't answer, son. You know I'd be very happy if . . ."

But George answered. He answered and answered! Her few words had lifted the lid of shyness. He suddenly began emptying his heart. A little embarrassed but more relieved, he told her about Bettina–and at the same time he explained in detail his plans for Renni.

Mother Marie showed not the least surprise. She knew the sweetness and strength of George's character. She could trust him. She had taken his silence and reserve exactly as she now took his full confidence–as a matter of course. She petted Renni. All she said was, "He's so clever. If you keep on being patient, you two will manage it together."

Nothing more was said then of Bettina. But a few evenings later just before they went to bed, Mother Marie suddenly remarked, "I'd like to know her." George knew whom she meant.

He consulted Bettina. Then he reported to his mother. "She can't get up the courage to come."

Mother Marie said nothing. She thought she understood this gentle girl.

Chapter VIII

THE SWEET IDYLLIC LIFE GEORGE was leading curved toward exciting and even stormy events.

There was the scene with Karl. There was the meeting with the man who had been cheated. But it was the arrival of the Russian family that stirred things up most.

Once again George went to visit old Vogg. He was witness to a violent scene between the dog-breeder and Karl.

As George went in, Vogg was saying, "You shall never have Pasha again. Here's your money. We're through with each other." He spoke quietly but with suppressed, angry power. Pasha was lying abjectly on the floor. Karl began yelling at the top of his voice.

"We are not through, not by a long shot, not by a very long shot. I bought the dog and paid for him. Do you understand? He's my property."

Vogg replied, still quite calm. "Bought? Yes. On condition that you treat him properly."

"I do. Of course I do," Karl stormed.

"No," insisted Vogg, and now his voice was trembling. "No, the whip in your hand is witness against you. The use you make of it, the all-too-frequent use . . ."

"You can't be the judge of that. Not you!" Karl was scornful.

The breeder smiled grimly. "That's precisely what I can judge. I'm just the man to judge it. I can judge it a great deal better than you. That timid way of Pasha's is full proof how right I am."

"So," mocked Karl, "I suppose I'm to learn from you

how to treat a dog. You've certainly got the big head."

"It's of the utmost indifference to me whether you want to learn or not." Vogg was quite calm on the surface. "As a matter of fact, I suppose no one *learns* to be humane. It's something you have by nature–like this man here." He pointed to George. "Either a man has a heart–as he has–or he's a brute like you!"

"So, you call me a brute?" spat out Karl. "You shall be a witness," he growled at George.

"I'm not calling you anything," was the answer. "I'm simply making a statement about your character."

"You'll answer for this insult in court." Karl was shouting again.

"Very willingly," agreed Vogg. "I'll answer for anything I say. In any case, you've not fulfilled the conditions I laid down, and so I declare the sale off. Here's your money. If you don't take it I'll deposit it with the proper authorities."

Karl roared in his rage. "You foreign hound! Who are you to make the laws? You'll find out who's master here!"

Now the breeder was getting enraged. "Don't scream," he commanded, gritting his teeth. "You're making a fool of yourself. I'd like to remind you that you're in my house."

Karl stopped. Vogg went on talking louder and louder. "A foreigner, am I? Perhaps. But I'm no foreigner to justice and humanity. You call me a foreigner? Get out! At once. Or . . ." He walked up to his opponent and raised his fist.

George was ready to throw himself between them, but Karl, suppressing his anger, turned to the door. "Come, Pasha," he muttered.

The dog leaped as though on a spring.

"Stop!" thundered Vogg. He caught Pasha by the collar and pulled him over to the desk. "The dog stays here!"

Karl ran out, slamming the door behind him so that it cracked like a pistol shot.

"Well, old boy," laughed Vogg, petting Pasha, who hardly dared wag his tail, "well, you're free from your torturer." He turned to George. "That fellow's a rascal, isn't he?"

"How did it all start?" asked George.

"What he wanted here I really don't know. Evidently I was supposed to admire his kind of training. No, thank you. Not in my line. He ordered the dog to lie down, in that harsh way of his. That was the first thing I didn't like. I wanted to encourage the poor creature; I spoke to him in a friendly way. Pasha made only the slightest motion to come to me. And then that swine struck him such a blow with his whip that the poor dog howled. It riled me through and through, but I pulled myself together and calmly counted out the money he had paid me. At first he couldn't understand what I was driving at. When I patiently explained, he began to rave. You know the rest."

"It's perfectly clear to me, Mr. Vogg, that you're in the right–according to the way we look at things. Whether you can defend it in court if he brings an action for the recovery of the dog, I'm very doubtful."

The old man turned pale. "That's the fault of the laws–they're so easy on people who abuse animals," he broke out. He was now much angrier than he had been before. He walked up and down, waving his arms. " The law! The law!" he cried. "Blast the law! It doesn't afford near enough protection for harmless creatures. Not near enough."

He drew a deep breath, passed both hands over his face, bent down, petted Pasha gently on the back. The dog accepted the caress without a sign.

Then Vogg greeted Renni. "Well, sir, you are getting along all right, aren't you?" Renni, who had been a little frightened at the tumult, became happy instantly. He leaped on his master and then on Vogg. Vogg took him by the paws, looked into his serious eyes. "Yes, yes, old man, we're fighting for your kind. We won't let anything bad happen to you." Turning Renni loose, he asked George, "What brings you to my house?"

"Nothing special," answered George. He had to stop and collect his thoughts. He had just wanted to visit Vogg again, and he had something to tell him about the progress of his training.

"Without any punishment at all?" the old man asked.

"Without the least punishment," George assured him.

"Well now, a little lick once in a while–that might do some good and it could hardly harm the dog. I could trust you for that."

"No," insisted George. "I don't dare. You see, I've got Renni used to one kind of treatment. If I tried 'a little lick or two,' the effect might possibly be too violent, too far-reaching." As Vogg smiled he grew more earnest. "There have been a few times when I've been very much tempted to give Renni one or two. I admit that." Vogg's smile grew broader and Renni looked questioningly from one to the other. "But," said George, "I made up my mind to complete the training entirely without punishment, without any violence whatever, or else give it up altogether."

"I'll have to be shown," remarked the old man sceptically. "It would be a most unusual case, and so might prove nothing at all."

"It would be an object lesson for men in their dealing with animals," said George triumphantly.

Vogg persisted, smiling good-naturedly. "Most unusual I'd call it."

• • •

Downstairs in front of the house George, to his surprise, found Karl walking up and down, snorting with rage. "I was waiting for you," he cried. "We haven't seen each other for a long time. Where have you been keeping yourself, anyway?"

He did not wait for George's stammered excuses. "Naturally you're on the side of that old fool," he spluttered, and thundered on without heeding George's attempted reply. "Don't say a word. I know exactly what a sentimental weakling you are. I know too that you've been avoiding me. It makes no difference to me. Do you imagine you have a monopoly on loving animals? You're crazy! As if I didn't love my Pasha! *My* Pasha, I said. Yes, *mine*. He belongs to me!"

He snorted again. "Now that Pasha is an almost perfectly trained police dog, now that I've accomplished all I have with him, the old idiot has to interfere with his fool show-off. But I'll make an example of him. The old thief! He wants to steal my dog, but I'll give him something to remember me by!"

Before George could think of anything to say in Vogg's defence, there came an interruption. Pasha suddenly burst out of the door in a headlong run, caught sight of Karl, circled around him once, swinging his tail for joy, and, with his body arched in pleasure, went through the elaborate ceremony of finding his master.

"Hello! There you are again." Karl let out a peal of triumphant laughter. All his anger had evaporated. "Here, Pasha," he ordered, and snapped the leash to his collar. A "that will do" put a quick end to any further show of exuberant feeling. Again and again interrupted by his own laughter, he said to George, "The dog broke away from the old man. He knows where he belongs. It's the smartest thing he's ever done. I feel like standing on my head. Now let the old scoundrel have me arrested for cruelty to animals! Now let's see him annul the sale!"

George protested. "Vogg's not a rascal. He wouldn't steal your dog or anything else."

"That's an open question." Karl was now in complete good humour, satisfied with his victory, but still he did not want to give up the argument. "Question of how you look at it, old man. You're a sentimental soul and I'm made of sterner stuff, so let's not be enemies. Good-bye." He turned into a side street and strode off.

"Enemies!" thought George. As he looked after the stiffly marching form he could not get rid of a bitter feeling. He stood there uneasy and depressed.

The dog had made the decision. He had remained true to his master. Love for his tyrant had proved stronger than fear of abuse. Whoever tried to help him would only make himself laughing stock. George petted Renni, but this time the happy, trusting response brought no lift to his spirit. And so he went sadly home.

There lay Nemo, wretched and sick in the sun. He came to meet George, crawling painfully, humbly, on his belly, and again George could not decide whether the pitiful wreck of a dog was trying to beg forgiveness for something he had not done, or was once more trying to show gratitude for kindness. Here was another sacrifice to mankind's cruelty, thought George, stopping over to murmur a few gentle words and look into Nemo's sorrowful eyes.

"This outcast will go on mourning for the master he once had, and love him still in spite of everything. Oh, big-hearted dogs!" thought George. "Oh, mean-hearted men! Will it be so always?"

Mother Marie, after she had heard the story and realised how sad George was, comforted him. "Just go calmly along as you've been doing. Look at Vogg. He thinks as you do, and is working for the same end. Think about me–" she hesitated–"and about Bettina. Probably Nemo's owner was a drunkard. There are plenty of people in the world who have their hearts in the right place. You've happened to see two or three examples of cruelty. You think cruelty is everywhere. Well, there's far too much of it, I admit. It's rampant, here in Europe. We'll see lots more of it–nations for nations, races for races, men for animals, men against men. But we can be kind. We can do something with kindness. Don't set out to be a reformer. Don't make a martyr out of yourself. You weren't meant to be a martyr. You have a job to do, son. Keep cool." It was a long speech for Mother Marie.

Bettina, though not so wise in experience, was just as firm in her confidence. "The best thing would be to stop thinking about it. For after all there's nothing you can do to change some people."

Renni just put his forepaws on George's shoulders. There was nothing he could say.

PART II

Chapter IX

RENNI'S TRAINING HAD REACHED the point where it was really necessary to have someone play the part of a wounded soldier. Fortunately, just at this time the eccentric Russian family made their appearance. They had rented a large country house in the neighbourhood and set out to make their "get-acquainted" calls.

They came in two divisions. "If we all came at once it would be too many," declared Vassili Maximovich Safonoff, running his beautifully manicured hand through his long, full, grey beard. He talked slowly and solemnly as he introduced his wife Ludmilla. Her name was Ludmilla Philipovna, but his pet name for her was Millie. She was the exact opposite of her bear of a husband–short and plump and, where he was slow and solemn, active and gay. At least she was gay in her manner if not often in what she said.

Two beautiful young daughters made their best bows and kept respectful silence in the presence of their parents. All that could be learned of them was their names, Manya and Tanya. The moment Ludmilla caught sight of Renni she cried out eagerly, "That's the kind of dog I want! Big, strong watch dogs!"

"How many would you like, Millie?" inquired Vassili politely.

"Three or four would be enough." Ludmilla turned to Mother Marie. "Where can we buy dogs like that?"

The astonished George told her. Ludmilla got sight of Nemo. "Oh, the poor thing! It hurts me to look at him. Why do you let him live? You must kill him."

Ludmilla did all the talking. Mother Marie thought

her charming because she was so affectionate with the kitten. To be sure, her affection had been shown in words only, and at a respectful distance. Vassili treated Renni and Kitty with formal politeness, but he also kept at some distance. As they left he said, "Of course you will do us the courtesy of returning our call." He said it with the manner of a Czar, or at least a Grand Duke.

The next day the four young sons marched in. The eldest, Vladimir, about twenty-five, sat right down on the floor of the hall and began to hug poor Nemo. Sascha, the youngest–sixteen–excused him. "Don't get angry at my brother. He's only a child." Sascha already had all his father's pompous gravity.

His apologies were not needed. Vladimir had won the hearts of mother and son by his cordiality. They liked Mitya and Kolya, too. Mitya, a chubby fellow whose beard was beginning to grow, pressed Kitty close against his breast in spite of her scratching. The massive Kolya began tearing around the hall with Renni, and finally ran into the garden. The four Russian boys were as much at home as though they had long been intimate friends. Mother Marie and George soon recovered from astonishment and cheerfully accepted their free and easy manners. But George had a bad time getting their names straight and knowing which was which.

"Did Mama see the sick dog?" asked Vladimir, coming into the sitting-room.

George replied, "Yes, she thinks I ought to kill him."

Vladimir grinned. "That's just like *Mamitschka!* Her feelings are so tender, so easily touched!"

Before mother or son could express an opinion of this sort of sympathy, Vladimir suddenly bethought himself, leaped to his feet and bowed from the hips. "Oh, I beg your pardon! Good morning!" He grinned as he spoke. "Do you really think it's necessary to say 'Good morning'? I don't. Not at all. But *Papitschka* would certainly read me the riot act if I didn't." His disarming grin gave him an air of greatest innocence. There was a sort of magic attraction about him.

Soon, with visits back and forth, a real friendship was cemented. The family had left Russia before the end of the World War and had succeeded in saving their fortune. All the children except Vladimir had been born in foreign countries, but the Safonoffs had managed to keep their Russian birthright. Icons, samovars, bows of politeness, a readiness to confide and be close friends on short notice–everything remained truly Russian. There was a rumour that old Safonoff was a prince. He made no use of his title. The only sign of his rank was his heavy, elaborate dignity, which seemed born in him.

George got along with them swimmingly. He couldn't find much to say to stiff, taciturn Manya; but to make up for it he grew very friendly with the lovely Tanya, who was cheerful like her mother, and whom he liked better and better. Tanya petted Renni till he became her abject slave. She was very polite to Mother Marie, and she would pin up her skirts and go out into the garden to help George.

George explained to the four Russian brothers his plans for Renni's education. They became enthusiastic at once and offered to play wounded. It struck them all as a new, fascinating kind of game, and they could hardly wait to begin.

Vladimir had a wonderful gift as a whistler. He was also an accomplished musician. He could sit at a piano and improvise Russian songs, whistling the melodies in long-drawn melancholy, sweet-sounding tones. George did not have a piano, so they had to content themselves with Vladimir's whistling unaccompanied. As soon as he began Renni would come up to him, lay his head on his knee and listen raptly, as though he could follow the beautiful melodies.

Now they went out into the field, into the forest. The four brothers went first, by themselves. They chose positions at some distance from one another and stretched out on the ground, as George had told them to do. A little while later he followed with Renni, and then he met Bettina.

"If the dog knows the men, it will be easier, and yet at the same time it will be harder." In her matter-of-fact way of looking at things, she had hit on the truth.

Renni had already learned how to quarter a field, to cut back and forth across it, to circle it. At a word from George, or a mere sign, he had been taught to strike out, back and forth across the field, in the brush and in the woods. But every time he returned to his master, either of his own accord or at a call, he had worn a puzzled air as though he wanted to ask, "Why? What's this all about?" For in spite of his systematic searching and hunting there was nothing to be found. It had seemed to him perfectly useless and without object. It baffled him. George had been going at the task in quite a different manner from the ordinary training methods.

Now they were ready to get down to business.

"Find!" he ordered. Renni was off in a gallop, dropped into a quick trot, charged back and forth. The breeze brought him a well-known scent. He started out to follow it and ran straight toward its source. Much to his surprise he found Vladimir lying on the ground in the forest, fell on him joyfully, was received cordially and lavishly petted. The two played and romped together. When they had to get up and go to George, Renni's face wore an air of triumph.

"No good!" pronounced George.

Bettina added, "I knew it."

"How do you mean, no good?" Vladimir asked. "Renni found me, didn't he?" He too wore an air of triumph, comically like the dog's.

"Yes, but you spoke to each other."

"Why, of course we did," admitted Vladimir, petting Renni's back. "Of course we did. We were glad to see each other. Smart dog."

"If you're going to act like a wounded man, or a sick man who's lost consciousness, you couldn't do anything worse, anything more stupid, than what you've done," explained Bettina.

Vladimir looked at her for a second, then he grinned good-naturedly and answered, "Excuse me! What should I have done? I know I'm an ass."

Bettina smiled without replying. George suppressed a laugh. Renni in delight was running from one to another. Vladimir whispered to him, "We made fools of ourselves, we two." Renni didn't seem altogether crushed, and Vladimir was not suffering from too much remorse.

They called the other three brothers out of the woods and started home.

"It's a beginning," comforted George. "You mustn't take it so seriously."

He might have spared his words. Nobody seemed to be taking it seriously. Vladimir was walking with Bettina. George and the other three along behind. The Russian boys had met Bettina before and taken a liking to her. Now they came to the crossroad where Bettina usually said good-bye. Vladimir, who knew how matters stood, would not permit it this time. Grinning in his nice, friendly fashion, he grew suddenly insistent. "You might just as well stop being an idiot, my dear. I mean what I say. Your bashfulness is idiotic. Mother Marie has invited you to her house, and you don't come. You're insulting the good lady."

Bettina was not allowed to defend herself. Her excuse that she lacked the courage he refused to consider. "With a bodyguard of five men, you've nothing to fear. Seriously," he added, "do you want to conceal how you and George feel about each other?"

Surprised and embarrassed, Bettina could not think up an answer. So she came to George's home with a good deal more of a fanfare than she would have liked. At first she was quiet and shy, but the four brothers kept laughing and showing off, and Renni raced around in an outburst of high spirits. She began to relax.

Mother Marie greeted her very simply. "I've known of you for a long time and am very happy to see you in my house."

Tanya, who had just come in, said cordially, "I'm so glad you're here!"

"This is my sister Tanya," cried Vladimir. He stepped up to Mother Marie, kissed her on the cheek and whispered, "Thank you." No one else could hear him because Sascha, Kolya and Mitya were all yelling in unison, "What does he mean by *his* sister? He thinks he's the whole show. He wants Tanya all for himself."

They sat down and discussed the unsuccessful rehearsal. Slowly and pompously like his father Sascha declared, "Vladimir ought not to have been the first to lie down for Renni to find. No, sir. It is an accident, a sheer accident, that he is the oldest of us brothers.

Age should have nothing to do with it. He is really an infant, with that everlasting grin of his."

Vladimir grinned obligingly. "I am an ass. Bettina found that out first thing, and told me so to my face."

Amid general laughter Bettina tried to deny it. She blushed like a peony.

"Tomorrow I'll be the wounded man." Chubby Mitya laid down the law.

Sure enough, the next day Mitya lay in the tangled bushes. He had picked out the place himself. After an eager search Renni found him and wanted to go through all the to-do of a happy reunion. But Mitya kept his eyes closed, and just gave a low groan once in a while. At first the dog was completely stumped. He pawed around at Mitya and seized him by the coat collar with careful teeth as if to help him to his feet. Then he lay down beside the motionless man, whimpering softly.

At last, as though struck by a sudden idea, he tore away as fast as he could run. In a straight line he made for George, sprang up on him barking impatiently, pulled at his coat, ran ahead a few steps, wheeled about so as not to lose him and to urge him to hurry. Then he ran on again a few steps, only to repeat the performance. In this way he led his master to Mitya. Then they went through the business of giving the wounded man first aid; as he slowly "came to," Renni sat on his hind quarters watching the whole procedure closely. At last Mitya raised up painfully. The dog seemed to understand it all. He whirled about them, swinging his tail, but not until George had praised him most heartily and Mitya had stammered a few words of make-believe gratitude, did he give vent to an outburst of joy. Bettina petted him whenever she could get her hands on him–which, with all his high spirits, was seldom.

George wanted to send Renni out again, but Mitya said, "Enough for today."

Bettina too was of that opinion. "Be satisfied with this great success for the first real trial."

So George gave the signal and one after another the three brothers came out of the woods. Vladimir grinned, "Was it no good again?" He and Kolya were surprised and gratified to hear that things had gone so well. They were lavish in petting Renni and congratulating George.

But Sascha spoke gravely to Renni. "Yes, yes. You are a fine dog indeed." Then he turned to George. "I beg you will excuse me from now on. I have something better to do than lie around in the woods all day."

At home they celebrated the event with a tea party to which the elder Safonoffs were invited. Only Manya and Sascha were absent. Father Safonoff wore an old-fashioned Prince Albert with the splendid, many-coloured rosette of some order shining in his lapel. He treated Bettina with elaborate politeness in which there was a very little, barely noticeable condescension. Mother Safonoff examined her carefully through her lorgnette and was distinctly cool. To Renni, the hero of the day, she said a few nice words, but she did not touch him when he came up to her.

"I never touch animals with my bare hand," she declared. "I wish my children would take an example from me."

Old Vassili was not strictly bound by this notable example. He ventured to tap Renni with the fingertips of his left hand in order to ward off his over-friendliness. "Now, now, that is all right. Go on, now." Then he pulled out his handkerchief and carefully wiped the tips of his fingers, looking the while at his wife, who smiled indulgently.

"I knew all the time, son," said Mother Marie, "that your patience would do it."

"And Renni's smartness," added George, beaming with happiness.

"Bettina deserves more credit than anyone else," said Vladimir, and then he asked, grinning broadly, "Why are you blushing, Bettina?"

She did not answer.

Ludmilla could scarcely wait until Bettina had gone. "Who is that impossible person? I simply cannot stand her."

In the embarrassed silence Tanya said, "Why?"

"Because she tries to use her charms on people, the shameless thing."

Vladimir grinned. "But, *Mamitschka* . . ."

That was as far as he got. His father broke in. "I sincerely hope you are not presuming to contradict your mother."

It was said solemnly, with a slight threat in the tone. Vladimir stammered something unintelligible, lowered his head and fell silent. Mother Safonoff looked around with a smile of triumph. But Mother Marie proposed to show her how tactless she had been.

She said, very decidedly, "Bettina would not be my guest if I had any occasion to think her designing or bold. You are mistaken, dear lady, very much mistaken. She is a modest and well-behaved young girl who is looking for work, and I'm thinking of giving her work in my house."

"Ah, a servant." Ludmilla's laugh was painful and betrayed her vexation over the lesson she had received.

"Call it what you please." Mother Marie was smiling now. "A servant, if you wish. Here in our country all good people are equal, and there is nothing dishonourable or undignified about being a servant."

"We are no longer in Russia, Millie," came Vassili's booming, gloomy organ tones.

She sighed deeply. "Alas, alas!"

Chapter X

RENNI'S EDUCATION WAS MAKING swift progress now. The next time he went out he located two of the brothers, Mitya and Vladimir, and later on, all three, Kolya, Mitya and Vladimir. (Sascha was not again to be lured into this child-play, so beneath his dignity.) Again and again Renni went through the strange experience of finding his friends lying sick and helpless, and of having them recover with astonishing speed as soon as he brought George along to help. At times he got so confused he didn't know what to do when he came on Mitya or Vladimir motionless and suffering. He would just lie down by them, stretch out and whimper. They would leave him in his grief until after a while he would remember his duty and dash away like an arrow.

Slowly the dog came to understand that he must aid them, must save them. As Bettina had predicted, the friendship with the Russian brothers had proved at once a hindrance and a help. George devoted himself more and more to the dog's training. He went at the practising so eagerly that he neglected his garden and his field. But Bettina was there now. She worked busily at Tanya's side.

She had been unable to withstand Mother Marie's persuasion, well seconded by Tanya. The two had grown all the more enthusiastic over Bettina as a result of Ludmilla's unjust and unkind remarks. So Bettina lived at the house, slept in the attic room, ate with them at the table like one of the family, and worked busily from morning till late at night.

"You're doing more for George when you help out

here at home than if you went along to train the dog," said Mother Marie.

From the start Tanya talked with Bettina as if they had been the most intimate friends. "Leave George alone with Renni," she would say. "He won't even miss you. He's like a man possessed. Here you can really be useful to him." Which was the truth if not altogether flattering. Absorbed in the dog, he forgot the girl. George had had nothing to do with her coming, barely noticed her at home, did not miss her at all when he was at the training. Bettina's help in the house he seemed to take as a matter of course. Once he defended himself briefly to his mother.

"It won't be very long now until I have to join the colours for manœuvres, and then of course I can't work here. I hope by then to have Renni so far along that I can take him with me and report him for duty."

Vladimir developed a sudden interest in the garden and field work. He helped cut vegetables and salads, pulled turnips, gathered tomatoes from the frames, picked red currants, and kept an eye on the peaches and apricots, getting rid of insects. He made up chrysanthemums and asters–his favourite flowers–into great bouquets, dealt, grinning as usual, with the people who came to buy, and spent as much time as possible near Bettina. He disregarded Tanya's quizzical smile.

Now out in the forest something very important happened, something which George hailed as final and positive proof of the success of his training. They were going contentedly home one day. Renni had found all three of the carefully concealed brothers, one right after the other, and each time had rushed up at full speed to get George. Mitya was saying, "We've gone the limit. He knows us too well. We mustn't keep on or he'll get to the point where he won't believe there's anything wrong with us."

"That's right," replied George. "It would be a good idea to use strangers. But where shall we find them? As far as the dog's losing faith is concerned, if that's what you're afraid of, I don't think you need worry.

Dogs believe everything we tell them, blindly. If I put my hands in front of my face and act as if I were going to cry, Renni's sympathy immediately throws him into greatest distress. As soon as I take my hands away and begin to laugh, he's at once beside himself for joy."

Big Kolya put in, lazily, "He thinks it's all just a game." Mitya suggested that everything was a game to Renni.

"That's a mistake, a great mistake," contradicted George. "Why would he get so desperate over my crying? Doesn't he come rushing from each of you as though, if I delayed for a minute, you might be in dire danger? No, you must get into your heads what unlimited trust and confidence dogs give us. We're their gods."

Vladimir grinned. "You a god, George? Remarkable!"

"You too," answered George quietly. "All of you are gods in Renni's eyes."

"We're a gob of gods," fat Mitya remarked dryly. "I'm Jupiter. Who are you?" They all laughed.

"Renni still has much to learn," declared George firmly. "A very great deal."

"What else?" Kolya wanted to know.

"Well, for instance, the way to make his report, how to bring stimulants and first-aid kits, but, most important of all, how to behave under fire. Just think–machine guns, cannon, hand grenades, bombs."

"They're no trifling matter," said Vladimir and for the first time failed to smile.

Just at this moment Renni stopped dead still, his ears high, and sniffed anxiously toward the forest. Then suddenly making up his mind he struck out straight ahead through the brush.

"Call him back, why don't you?" demanded Kolya.

"No, let him have his fun," smiled Vladimir.

"I don't believe he ran off for fun," Mitya argued.

"Let's wait," George said. He seemed rather nervous. They all waited in silence, sharing his uneasiness. It was quite a while before Renni came back. Excited and almost beside himself, he urged George to come at once and help. As usual he ran ahead a few steps, whirled around and looked back to see if George were following, then ran on a little and did it all over again. The others stayed behind.

"Somebody must have had a serious accident," said Vladimir. "That would be simply wonderful!"

Mitya said, "The fellow who had the accident would hardly agree with you," and naturally this brought out Vladimir's delightful grin.

The dog led his master deep into the forest. There, half-hidden under a hazel bush, lay a boy of about fifteen, moaning and moaning. George could hear him quite a way off. When he stood over the boy, he said, "What's the matter?"

The answer came in a whimper. "I don't know. I must have fallen over a tree trunk or a root. I can't get up. My ankle's broken or sprained."

"How do you come to be in the woods alone?"

"I was hunting mushrooms. Oh! Ouch!"

"Is the pain very bad?"

"It's terrible." The boy bent double. Stooping over him George lifted his left leg. The boy screamed when he touched the ankle.

"The shoe must come off," said George.

"No, no. Please don't," wailed the boy. But George got

out his knife and, in spite of the cries of pain, carefully cut the shoe from the ankle. It was terribly swollen. The pain eased a little, but the boy groaned, "Now I'll have to run around barefoot. I won't have any shoes now."

"Well, old man, you can't run anyhow with that ankle, and by the time you're walking again I'll give you a new pair of shoes."

When the sock had been removed the thick swollen joint was a dark blue from the ruptured blood vessels.

"Quiet now. We'll soon have you out. I can't carry you alone." George hurried off. His heart was beating violently, he was so excited over what Renni had done all by himself. It sent him clear up in the air with joy to note how the dog, who had followed him, kept looking back worriedly toward the boy. When he came out onto the glade, he could no longer hold in.

"Good work, old boy!" he cried, taking Renni's head in both hands. "You've learned your lesson perfectly. I'm pleased with you–more than pleased. I'm as happy as can be."

The dog waved his plume eagerly, but still seemed

set on going back. Mitya interrupted the praise. "Well, did somebody have an accident?"

"Yes," cried George, exultant. "Just think what all this means. I've reached the goal of all my efforts, and I've reached it through patience and kindness, and the wonderful intelligence of my dog. Nothing else. . . ."

Again Mitya broke in. "And the injured man? Are you going to let him lie there, or is he already dead?"

"Heavens, no!" George, who had been almost drunk with happiness, came to his senses. "Certainly not. Come with me. Quick!"

"Renni is already ordering us to come," said Vladimir.

The dog rushed into the bushes as soon as he saw them start out. George answered the other's questions. "A poor boy. He was looking for mushrooms, and he broke his ankle, or at least sprained it."

"Which foot?" asked Mitya.

"I haven't the slightest idea."

Kolya put in, "How stupid!" But it wasn't clear whether he referred to Mitya being so precise, or George being so unattentive. Talking loudly they fought their way through the bushes. As they strung along behind Renni, they praised him according to their several natures. Mitya said he had known from the dog's manner that he had it in him, or he never would have wasted time on all those tests. That set Vladimir grinning again.

They found the youngster almost out of his head with pain. He could not defend himself from Renni's affectionate greeting, or push him away when he insisted on washing his face with his tongue. They carried him out to the road, while he whimpered and stammered, "Good old dog," and "He's my guardian angel. My rescuer." As soon as the road would permit it, the four of them raised him on their shoulders. They did not have to carry him far, for a woman who came along undertook to call the hospital. So they laid the patient down in the grass at the roadside. George inquired his name and address. He was Rupert Fifer, the son of a tailor, and he lived in the workers' district. He did not have a bit of money. George gave him some and promised again to see about the shoes. Each of the three brothers gave him money, too. The boy grew almost cheerful.

At last the ambulance arrived. Young Doctor Britt introduced himself and examined Rupert, who was crying piteously. The ankle was broken. Amid his groans the doctor put on a first-aid bandage and ordered him to the hospital. Vladimir told the crowd that had gathered how and by whom the boy had been found. After Rupert had been placed in the ambulance Mitya stepped over to him.

"I'll get word to your father at once," he said shortly.

"Thank you," moaned Rupert.

They could still hear him groaning, "Thank you for everything," as the ambulance drove away.

The crowd staged a little ovation for the dog and for the young men, before it scattered. A fat, rather elderly gentleman said, "A dog like that proves mighty useful."

George and the brothers started home.

"That was Renni's first taste of publicity," grinned Vladimir.

George, a bit pale from excitement and nervousness, couldn't say a word.

"I'm going to the tailor's at once," said Mitya, and, without saying good-bye, started down a side street. Kolya approved. "The boy's our find. We must take care of him."

"Find?" Vladimir smiled. "That's a funny word, find."

At home they celebrated the incident like a solemn festival. Mother Marie and Bettina set the tea table, Tanya went for her parents, and soon they were all seated. Manya and Sascha did not honour the occasion with their presence.

The hero of the day was, of course, Renni.

"He is really very remarkable," Ludmilla admitted graciously.

The dog no longer went near her, and this was probably one reason why she was coming to admire him. Vassili tapped him again with the fingertips of his left hand, murmuring, "You are really wonderful, wonderful beyond belief," at the same time pushing him away. "Now, now, that's enough. Go now." And then he rubbed his fingers hard with his handkerchief, exchanging a glance with his indulgently smiling wife.

In silence George drew Renni to his side. The dog sat down on his hind quarters, and George put an arm about him. Ludmilla watched through her lorgnette.

"I suppose you're feeling very proud of yourself now." George only shook his head in a puzzled way.

Tanya laughed. "One can be happy without being conceited."

And Vladimir said quizzically, "The dog's the only one who has reason to be stuck up, and he's just glad."

"Vassili, they're making out I'm rude," cried Ludmilla with a sort of wail, very much upset.

"You are mistaken, Millie." Vassili looked around with a rebuke in his glance, but his tone was solemnly mild. "Which of the children would, dear?"

Tanya and Vladimir put their denial into action. They rushed upon their mother, to hug and kiss her, smother her with caresses, call her endearing names, until Ludmilla, satisfied but quite out of breath, began to smile. She asked Bettina to bring her a glass of water, thanked her prettily, and even called her "my dear."

As a matter of fact, Ludmilla was a spoiled child

who would graciously swallow any amount of flattery. She had a grand opinion of herself, and was utterly naïve about it. She was as boundless in her claims on others as she was in her arrogance. But still she had charm. George had noticed it at once and had agreed with his mother when she said, "Oh, that Ludmilla! I'm so fond of her I can't resist her."

George had added, "That's just the way with me. Her children really love her wholeheartedly, but still they see through her. It is love without illusion."

The talk around the tea table veered back to Renni.

"All you need now is to go on repeating the same routine with him, so he won't get out of practice," said Mother Marie.

"You're right, but we've got to have strangers for him to go after."

Mitya reported on his visit to Rupert's father. The old man had not been at all frightened over his boy, but instead rather angry, and he had not calmed down till Mitya had engaged his two grown sons, Andrew and Rolf, to play "wounded" for a modest wage.

Mother Fifer, an angular, cross-grained person, had said, "Well, getting good pay with no work ought to suit you perfectly, you lazybones." She refused to go to the hospital. "Oh, rubbish! That Rupert! The rascal will be coming home as soon as he can limp again."

So this episode was settled in good order. The two Fifer lads played wounded with much dramatic talent. One day Bettina's brothers joined in and then they had wounded with a vengeance, so that it put quite a strain on Renni. But he went through with it without getting tired, eagerly and dependably.

At home he was still playful as before, tearing around frantically with Kitty. She would dare him on, spitting and arching her back, or else cuddle up close to his breast, purring contentedly. These diversions Renni seemed to regard as a sort of vacation.

Nemo became more and more solitary, more and more indifferent to all attempts to make friends with him, even to the friendliest words of the family—more dull and unresponsive. Bettina put words to it:

"The poor fellow won't last much longer."

No one answered. They felt she was telling the truth, but they did not like to agree with her and had not the courage to deny it.

Soon Renni learned to announce the finding of a wounded man without haste or excitement, without barking or pulling at his master's clothes. Merely by stretching out one paw.

"Now I'm sure I can take him along," said George, who was expecting from one hour to the next to be called up for manœuvres. "Now they'll just have to admit him to the Sanitary Corps."

Mother Marie, Bettina, Tanya and especially Vladimir, who these days was always in the field or the garden, declared unanimously that there was no possible doubt about Renni's being accepted. Mitya encouraged them still more.

"There'll be many a dog there who can't stand comparison with Renni." Everyone had confidence in young Mitya's positive judgments.

Chapter XI

NOW GEORGE HAD A TERRIBLE experience. For the first time in his life blind raging anger flamed in his breast. For the first time he felt tempted to a deed of violence.

He had been to see Rupert at the hospital, had found the young fellow free from pain and in the best of humours. Rupert inquired after Renni and said how very eager he was to see him again.

George asked, "Do you go to school?"

"I haven't for a long time," answered the boy and admitted honestly, "I don't want to study."

"Well then, what do you want to make of yourself?"

"Any kind of work would suit me if I could only get away from home."

George said he'd give him a chance to learn gardening. Rupert promised heartily to be industrious, steady, obedient.

On the way home George was planning this poor boy's education, when screams of pain suddenly startled him from his peaceful thoughts. Near by a dog was howling. Clearly he was being beaten with a stick or a whip. It was possible to tell each blow, for with each shriek of pain rose high, mingled with snarls of desperate pleading, and in the short pauses one could hear the low whimpering. George turned the next corner in a run and took in the scene. There stood a man beating a poor spaniel which writhed on the ground at his feet.

"You scoundrel!" George rushed on the man, tore the whip from his uplifted hand and cut him once across the face. It was a terrible blow. Again George shouted, "You wretch!"

The man lifted both hands to protect his head but made no resistance. He begged, "Don't! Don't!" The trace of the whip was a broad red line across his pale face–the face of a man just awakened.

"How do you like it?" muttered George. "It hurts, doesn't it?"

"Oh, frightfully," moaned the man, fingering the swollen welt. "But why strike me?"

"Why strike your dog, you scoundrel?" Suddenly George felt the spaniel leap against him, trying to bite him.

"Down, Karo," commanded his master. Karo dropped at once.

Again George's rage boiled up. "Aren't you ashamed to face your dog? You've just been treating him horribly, and still he tries to protect you."

"Yes." The man lowered his head. "Yes. I am ashamed. . . ." Sobs stifled his voice. He could speak only in jerks. "I am . . . so very . . . so terribly unhappy."

"Is your dog to blame for that?" George's anger cooled. He looked with curiosity at the pitiful figure before him.

"No," came the sobbing answer. "No, Karo's not to blame. He only . . . I can't even remember now what caused my outburst. I just meant to give him one blow . . . just one, really. But I got to thinking about her, and . . . something like a madness came over me."

"Thinking about whom?"

The man was weeping. "About Amalie, about my wife. She *was* my wife. But she ran away from me. She robbed me. All the money I'd saved up."

"When?"

"Two days ago."

"Report it to the police, why don't you? Go and have the thief arrested."

"Impossible," he whimpered. "She's gone away."

"Report her."

"No, I haven't the heart."

"But you have the heart to beat your friend half to death."

"My friend?"

"Don't act surprised. You know you have no better, more loyal friend than your poor dog."

The man was silent for a few seconds; then he sighed, "Yes, that's true." He knelt down. "Come here, Karo. You're the only friend I've got in the world. I know it. Come. I won't do anything to you." The spaniel took everything as if he had no will of his own. His master stroked the bruised body, fondled the splendid ears which hung long and silky like curls. "Please forgive me. We're unhappy, you and I. We've both been beaten, but I deserved it, you didn't."

The dog hesitated and then licked his master's hands and face.

"Is there a man on earth," asked George, "who if you had mistreated him like that would still be so grateful to you, so gentle?"

"No," he answered and straightened up. "None. You've showed me my only true friend. I thank you. Even if this spot does burn like fire." He pointed to his swollen face. "I've no other friend but him."

"If you're really sorry for what you've done count me your friend," said George, beginning to feel pity.

"Oh, please, please, don't leave me alone now."

They went along side by side, at first in silence; then the man began the story of his life. He spoke rapidly, helped by this chance to share his troubles.

He bore the curious name of Antony Flamingo. He was a bookkeeper in a large business house. A year and a half ago he had married, and he had scarcely had a day of peace since. The woman was vain, lazy, possessive; she constantly abused him, constantly demanded expensive luxuries. Because her serious-minded husband was unwilling to give her all his savings–they would hardly have lasted her a year–she had taken the money and cleared out.

"Even my name brought me bad luck. Flamingo. She ridiculed me for it. How can I help what my name is? I hate it."

"You're wrong. Flamingo is a beautiful name."

"It came from Spain. My great-great-grandparents were Spanish."

"Don't hate your fine name. Better hate your horrible wife. That might help you get over it. What's the sense in beating an innocent dog because of a person like that?" George was mounted on his hobby again and galloped off at full speed. Flamingo listened with growing astonishment. When George started in to prove that dogs are incapable of lying, he cried, "That's all my wife ever did–lie."

George told him what he had accomplished with Renni without a single blow. Flamingo wrung his hands. "I'm a monster." He bent down over Karo, patting the beautiful head of the still terrified spaniel. "I've treated you terribly, but there won't be any more of that now." Karo wagged the stump of his tail a little but seemed slow to trust this sudden kindness.

"Here," said Flamingo. "Here. You take the whip. I don't need it. I'll never touch my dog with it again."

As he handed the whip over to George, Karo shrank back terrified at the mere gesture.

"No, good old boy, nothing's going to hurt you," his master encouraged him. "Don't be afraid. Come on. Come here."

Obedient to the word of command the dog crept quivering under Flamingo's hands and then stood up surprised, reassured, happy merely to be petted.

George told about Karl, about the scene at Vogg's house and how Pasha had refused to be set free but had run after his tyrant out of pure love. Flamingo was now completely convinced and won over. Again he took hold of Karo and again Karo shrank from him.

"You love me, you, even if I have mistreated you. You love me in spite of it, don't you?" He patted the spaniel's back and neck awkwardly; it was easy to see his hand was not used to showing friendship to an animal. "You are true to me and will be true always. Now I know what loyalty is and where to find it."

When they came to say good-bye the cordial pressure of Flamingo's hand embarrassed George. The sight of the blood-red welt across his face hurt his conscience.

"Forgive me."

Flamingo was puzzled. "Forgive you? What for?"

"Why, you know, of course," stammered George.

"Oh, for that. For that I owe you a thousand thanks."

"You'll change your mind when you look in the mirror."

"Of course I won't."

"You'll have every right to."

"What are you thinking of? You . . ." He tried to go on speaking, but George interrupted him.

"I'm fearfully sorry. I can't even begin to tell you how sorry I am. I never did anything brutal in my life before. I can't forgive myself for being carried away like that."

Flamingo replied quickly. "Your regret . . . it's very nice but quite wrong. You've set me free. Really, you've changed my feelings entirely and I've won two friends. There's one"–he pointed to Karo–"and if it isn't presuming too much, you are the other."

They made arrangements to meet again, but it wasn't till long afterward and then unexpectedly, surprisingly, in altogether different circumstances, that they did so.

On his way home George thought of his mother's words about this unhappy Europe. Here was another instance of man's cruelty and greed–or woman's rather; of humiliation seeking relief in futile vengeance on the innocent. It would have to be a dog! And George thought of that reformer-martyr instinct in him that had got clear out of hand. He reproached himself bitterly for his own violent cruelty toward one individual who suffered from the disease of the incurable many. He had come out of it better than he deserved. He hung his head.

Chapter XII

AT HOME GEORGE FOUND THE order to report for manœuvres. He was to leave day after tomorrow. He took advantage of the day between to bring Renni to battalion headquarters.

The Sanitary officer took the animal by the muzzle.

"A beautiful dog," he said. He lifted Renni's lips and felt his teeth. "A fine dog. Only I'm afraid he's too young. He's barely a year old."

"He can do anything any other dog can do, if not more," George said.

"Come, come," smiled the officer. "Don't promise too much. Of what use can he be?"

"First aid, sir. He's perfect at finding sick or wounded men."

"So young–and so perfect? That would break records. Will you be responsible for it, Corporal?"

"Of course, Captain, entirely responsible."

Renni swung his tail as though the conversation pleased him and put his forepaws up on his master.

"Down," George said softly. The dog dropped to the ground instantly.

The officer was pleased. "He looks good," he said. "We'll give him a thorough trial. I'll detail you to the Red Cross first-aid service. You've had the regular rudimentary first-aid training yourself, of course?"

"Yes, sir, during last manœuvres. I got to be a corporal then."

The captain wrote a note, laid one hand on the dog's back and as he handed the paper to George, inquired,

"How about fire? Has he ever heard shooting?"

"Not yet, Captain." The captain looked thoughtful. George said earnestly, "Everyone has to begin some time, even a dog."

"It will be an experiment." The captain smiled again and said in a friendly way, "Dismissed."

George clicked his heels, saluted stiffly and withdrew. Not until he reached the steps did it occur to him that he ought to have said, "Thank you, sir." He was happy, yet a little uneasy. Fire . . . cannon . . . air bombs.

"How will you act when you see hell break loose, Renni?" he asked the dog, who looked up at him curiously. "Manœuvres are only half-war but even in half-war there's a good deal of shooting."

George took Renni to Vogg.

"Why did you send me that Russian jackass?" barked the breeder. "Think I'm running a wholesale business? You've got another guess coming!"

George was taken aback by this unfriendly reception. But when asked what caused it, Vogg only got gruffer.

"You know very well what that Russian wanted, or you wouldn't have sent him here. No, I'm through with you. It will be a lesson to me."

George insisted he did not know what he was talking about.

"Don't try your play-acting on me, you innocent lamb," Vogg growled. "I won't believe anything you say from now on. Your harmless Russian wanted to buy *three or four dogs!* Big dogs. Blazes! Why didn't he want my whole kennel? He wanted them for watch dogs! When I asked if he meant to keep them chained up, the old moss-back said without a blush, 'Of course I mean to keep them chained all the time.' I showed him out in a hurry. And you–what'll I do with you? Have I got to tell you how low-down it is to keep a dog chained? It's just hideous to take a fine, good-natured dog and make him surly, afraid of people, likely to bite. Don't you know there are decent ways to make a good watch dog?"

"Mr. Safonoff knows nothing about these things," George made bold to say.

Vogg blazed up again. "He knows nothing about

dogs–but he wants to buy three or four! He thinks money will do everything. He hasn't the slightest inkling of a dog's soul. He isn't even interested in it, the numskull! You can't do anything worse to dogs than fail to understand them. Merciful God! You can't teach some people anything. They think they know it all. Now I understand why you haven't been around here for so long."

"Oh, Mr. Vogg, there's no connection at all."

"No connection? Is that so!"

"No, really and truly. I've been busy with Renni's training, and now we're both detailed for Red Cross work."

"So soon? Congratulations." His tone was sarcastic. A side glance at Renni and a plainly audible murmur, "Poor fellow!"

"He isn't poor," protested George. "He's never needed anyone's sympathy."

Vogg laughed bitterly. "Go tell that fairy tale to your Russian uncle."

"I swear it. Not once."

"Certainly. I'm willing to take that oath as true. Literally. Not once, but a dozen times more likely."

Deeply hurt, George cried, "I swear that neither I nor anybody else has ever touched that dog."

"I don't believe it."

George's patience was at an end. "I was happy at the thought of bringing the dog to show you," he said quietly.

"I was happy and grateful. Since you insult me, I'd better be going."

As he closed the door behind him he heard Vogg's parting shot:

"Oh, go hang–"

That evening, the last before he joined his command, he spent at home, but it was spoiled by resentment. When he told his mother about the scene at Vogg's and made all sorts of guesses at what had happened between the breeder and old Safonoff, Mother Marie said, "Well, why don't you ask Vassili himself?"

George first tried Tanya and then Vladimir when

the Russians came to the house to say good-bye. Neither knew anything about it. So he mustered up courage and put it to the father direct, "You've not bought your watch dogs yet?"

Vassili slowly stroked his long white beard and, after a pause, replied solemnly, "No, not yet."

But Ludmilla explained, smiling sweetly. "We are certainly not going to buy any dogs from that ridiculous man. I really can't understand why you would recommend so rude a person. The ideas he has! The conditions he makes! As if he were giving us something! After all my husband told me about it I am convinced your friend is as big a fool as he is a ruffian."

Vladimir grinned. Vassili begged her with touching kindness, "Don't bother, Millie. Don't bother. We'll say nothing more about it. I assume George meant well."

With that the matter dropped. Indeed, it was almost cleared up.

Renni's appearance made a welcome diversion for most of those present. This evening even Manya and Sascha were in the company. Tanya petted Renni so tenderly that Manya, ordinarily taciturn though at heart very kind, broke out harshly, "Oh, quit it, Tanya. Don't carry on so."

Tanya blushed but did not answer.

Sascha growled, "Let Tanya carry on as much as she wants to. Stop your preaching."

Mitya took a hand. "Manya's always got to be bossy. And Tanya's as emotional as a girl in love."

A still deeper blush spread over Tanya's pretty face. Vladimir kept smiling.

"Don't quarrel, dear children," commanded Vassili gently.

"We aren't quarrelling, Father," Kolya said seriously. "We're just amusing ourselves."

They all burst out laughing.

Suddenly Ludmilla gave a shriek. Kitty with a sudden leap had landed on her shoulder. Vassili, completely taken aback, could only murmur, "For heaven's sake, Millie." Bettina hurried up and took the kitten in her arms.

"Thank you, thank you," smiled Ludmilla, again

quite pacified. "You have saved my life. Nobody is safe with all these animals around. Nothing can keep them from attacking you." She said it so cheerfully that her bite was easy to overlook.

Sascha said dryly, "Mama, you are talking nonsense."

"My son," Vassili began booming, but Sascha wouldn't let him say a word.

"Why, Mama knows she's talking nonsense. Renni never goes near her and poor old Nemo hasn't the strength to attack her. Evidently he doesn't want to anyway."

They laughed, but the laugh was a bit forced.

"You are unjust, Sascha." Vassili started to find fault but Sascha rudely shut him off again.

"Let me alone, please, Father. Nobody's going to stop me from expressing my opinions."

There was an appalled silence broken only by a sharp laugh from Manya. Then Ludmilla covered the painful situation. As though nothing had happened she cried out, "Oh, by the way, Renni–you have not killed him yet?"

George started. "Kill Renni? *Renni?*" He was hurt to the quick.

Ludmilla smiled sweetly. "Oh, of course I mean the other dog. The sick one. How is anyone to remember all these dogs' names?"

Vladimir grinned. "Two dogs' names. Only two." He got a stern look from his father, but he couldn't stop smiling as he thought: "Two dogs' names for her. Eight Russian names for them."

"We do not kill animals," Mother Marie declared. "At our house creatures are free to live their lives out to the end."

"That's funny," said Ludmilla, and Vassili repeated, "Very funny," at the same time shaking his head with a tragic air.

"Well," replied Mother Marie, "we're very funny then. Every human being is funny in some way, in his own way, and he doesn't even know it."

Then Vladimir started to whistle his sweet, sad Russian songs. His brothers and sisters chimed in with the words, but Vladimir's caressing, triumphant fluting soared above their voices. So the evening came to a musical end. Nobody paid any attention to Ludmilla, who shed a few tears and sighed, "Oh, my Russia!" Tanya and Vladimir were happy because George was again in a good humour and all took an affectionate leave of Renni—all except Ludmilla, Manya and Sascha. Even Vassili patted Renni on the back and Vladimir bent down to fondle him.

Chapter XIII

COMPLETELY EQUIPPED AND RIGHT on time George led Renni into the barracks. Five other dogs, each with his trainer, stood before the medical staff officer.

"Get your cur on the leash," he thundered to George.

"It isn't necessary, Captain. He'll not move from my knee."

"Do what I order you!" bawled the captain.

In silence George snapped the leash to the dog's collar.

"Now come over here and let me get a look at the beast."

George would have liked to reply that Renni was neither cur nor beast. But he kept silent, stepped up and handed the leash to the officer, who pulled Renni over to him very gently–a surprising gentleness. He examined Renni, petting him and speaking kindly. At the first glance at his teeth the captain blazed up. "Just what I thought! A puppy. How dare you bring a pup in here?"

George was irritated. His face flushed but he kept himself in control. "The Captain will see from the assignment slip I gave him that Renni has been accepted."

"Well, what do you expect to prove with that scrap of paper?"

"Only that I have not presumed."

"If the dog turns out no good . . . and I can tell that right now . . . I'll send you back to your regiment."

"The dog will prove himself."

"Silence!"

George was silent. He had perfect trust in his Renni. His comrades in the Medical Corps shook hands with him after they were dismissed and the dogs too exchanged friendly greetings, Renni the friendliest of all. His satisfaction at finding so many comrades was quite obvious. They were all police dogs, steady, well-fed, well-developed dogs perhaps four or five years old. One indeed was all of eight and there were white hairs on his muzzle. He was the calmest of the group, with that assurance which comes from experience. George saw on all the dogs' faces the serious look which had always delighted him when he caught it in Renni. The handler of the old dog, Sergeant-Major Nickel, spoke to George encouragingly:

"Why shouldn't your Renni be able to do the work? Nonsense! Just because he's young? My Hector was young too when he began. Of course, not quite as young as your dog. But that's just a way the old fussbudget has of showing his importance." He jerked his shoulder scornfully in the captain's direction. The latter was busy detailing the stretcher-bearers and the dog-handlers, whom he assigned according to a prearranged list. Three bearers and a dog-handler to each battalion.

"Be sure to remember your assignments," he warned. "They'll be the same in case of war unless–" he looked at George meaningly–"unless there's a change made first."

"Very well, sir," growled Nickel with a tinge of scorn in his voice.

One after another started off with the stretcher-bearers.

"You have the farthest to go," a comrade cried to George as he hurried past.

"Double quick!" roared out the commander behind them. "That means you. This is no Sunday stroll."

"Come, Renni," George said softly and darted off. Renni kept step with him but did not pull at the leash, did not pant, held to a steady gait. They reached their battalion, took their position behind the ranks. The three bearers patted Renni, who accepted their caresses calmly.

"A beautiful animal," said one.

Another had news. "Likely we'll see action before the day's over."

"Where?" asked the third. "The enemy's a long way off."

"Enemy?" thought George. "Renni and I shall have no enemies, even in war."

"Battalion, forward march!" The mass of men began to move.

"Where's the band?" someone asked.

"Ass!" was the answer. "These manœuvres are on a war footing. There won't be any band."

Another added, "Oh, well. When we start home there'll be plenty of that oompah-oompah-oomp."

From the air overhead came the mighty hum of propellers from a squadron of planes. Renni lifted his head.

"There's your music," laughed someone.

"Those are our planes," another cried.

Renni was still looking up in astonishment. George was on the point of saying, "Quiet, old boy," but it wasn't necessary. Renni was quiet. He had only given way to his curiosity for a few seconds.

"When we get to the woods," came a voice from the rank and file, "once we get to the woods, we won't have to march in close rank any longer."

Another voice corrected him. "Maybe we'll deploy sooner than that."

Two hours passed. Three. March, march, march. The heat was getting oppressive. Suddenly there came a crash from in front, rather close. Anti-aircraft batteries. George looked anxiously at his dog. Renni pricked up his ears just once, but that was all the note he took of the artillery thunder. Again came the whirring of motors in the air–this time from the opposite direction, and this time Renni gave no sign whatever that he noticed them.

"Skirmish lines! Skirmish lines! Deploy!" came the order. "Rifles ready! Forward!"

In the twinkling of an eye the close-packed mass dissolved, scattered and, as it dipped into the forest, became invisible. Now the cannon began to roar, shaking the earth with explosions, but not shaking Renni's calm.

"Fine, old boy! Fine! Better than I ever expected." George could not keep from hugging him.

"Artillery preparation," said a soldier. "The order to charge will come soon."

From far away came the deep booming of the howitzers. The machine guns clattered sharply.

"I'd never have thought the fun would start so soon." Some man screamed the words at the top of his voice, but with all the uproar he could hardly be heard.

"Soon!" cried another. "You idiot! The fun's been going on for hours."

"Charge!" cried a voice of command. And "Charge!" was repeated down the line.

The drums whirred the charge. The trumpets blew the charge. As though carried along by a storm wind the force whipped on, a column of tanks at their head, hurling lightning; another column of tanks came to meet them, spitting flame. Renni in the midst of all this madness seemed utterly unconcerned. The infernal nerve-shattering racket left him perfectly cool. All of a sudden he stopped, sniffed the air, pulled the other way. George unsnapped his leash and Renni raced off.

After a little while he led George to a soldier who had fainted and was lying unconscious on the ground. By the time the three stretcher-bearers had given him a stimulant Renni was off in another direction. He hurried swiftly back, urging George at the double quick to a sick man who was writhing in agony. Renni was quartering the ground here, there, everywhere. A major taking part in the charge called out, "Whose dog's that? He's too smart." A number of soldiers pointed to George.

"You, there. Don't you hear me? Why don't you call your dog back?"

"I can't do that. The dog has spotted something and he's doing his duty."

"Duty? Any wounded man ought to hold out till there's a pause in the fighting," croaked the major.

The two of them were roaring at each other like mad, to make themselves heard above the tumult of the mock battle.

"The Major must know that in a real fight there'd be badly wounded men who'd need help in a hurry."

"My dear fellow," the major growled, "neither you nor your dog would live long in a real fight."

George shrugged his shoulders. Renni gave him no time to answer. He was off and George must follow.

"That dog won't let any fellow that's hurt go without attention," cried a soldier in the major's ear. "I never saw such a dog."

"He'd be a sure candidate for death if the thing were serious," shrieked the major.

"It would be too bad if he got killed," the soldier grumbled to himself.

The charge went on. It seemed marvellous to George as he watched Renni slip between the rushing, fighting lines and get in no one's way. How careful he was not to let George out of his sight, while at the same time he urged the stretcher-bearers on. Everyone who saw the racing dog gaped at him.

"That's not a dog at all. He's greased lightning," they said, or, "He's a regular Brother of Mercy," or, "He's got more courage than most men."

Renni found five more exhausted men in all the mêlée.

Twilight rolled its deep veils of shadow over the earth. Finally the trumpet sounded, "Cease firing!" The thunder of artillery stopped instantly, the planes vanished from the sky, and only here and there a rifle shot resounded. Everything grew quiet. A silence brought to life by the now audible talking of the men. Nobody knew which army had been judged winner of the day. Nobody cared. Tired and thirsty as they were, their thought was only of food and drink, and they hailed with loud hurrahs the kitchen wagons which were attached to each company.

Renni, however, did not seem to have his mind on food. He scarcely noted the words of his master, and acknowledged his praise only by a brief swing of his tail. He stiffened, sniffed attentively into the dark, vanished. After a while he came back and begged George to come along. He ran ahead with short steps so as not to lose his master in the dark. By his leading George came on a boyish young lieutenant who had collapsed from thirst. Revived with some water and a few lumps of sugar the young man, much ashamed of himself, recovered enough to stagger off to his troop with George's help.

"Fine dog," he kept whispering. "Good dog."

Even yet Renni was not ready to rest. He went on

running back and forth across country, stopping, sniffing. Then he staged a seal feat. Without going first to investigate he urged his master and the stretcher-bearers to come with him. After quite a way the four men heard the very, very low moaning that the dog had caught long before. At last they bent over an unconscious man who had fallen and seemed to have injured himself seriously. All four helped carry him. Renni, well pleased with himself, strolled along behind. The man was bleeding from a wound on the head. One of the bearers ran off for a surgeon.

The whole troop–that is to say, all who were awake–came out to meet Renni. They crowded around him, overwhelmed him with praise. They brought him food and water. Renni, whose tongue was hanging out, drank eagerly and long, ate a very little and lay down on the ground.

"Now I know what it means to be 'dog-tired,'" said a sergeant-major in heartfelt tones.

"Well, old boy," George asked, "are we through for today?"

Renni wagged his tail. George stretched out beside him. Both were instantly asleep.

The man with a head wound had been sent off in an ambulance, but they did not hear it. Nor did they hear the major when he came by and inquired, "Where's that eighth wonder of the world?"

"Sh, sh!" they said. "He's sleeping."

To be sure, Renni raised his head for a second, but nobody noticed it, and he went to sleep again instantly. He did not hear the major's whispered words, "Let him sleep. He's earned it and he certainly needs it."

Chapter XIV

VERY EARLY, LONG BEFORE daybreak, the second day's manœuvres began. As silently as possible the troops lined up. They slipped in loose formation up under the mountain and, in the pale light of breaking day, tried to climb the steep slope before them without being observed. They were almost completely successful. The whole regiment had all but reached the heights when the first burst of fire came from the enemy cannon massed there. The thunder of the guns grew louder and louder. Immediately their own artillery laid down a barrage like a protecting storm. The regiment charged with irresistible fury, and the umpire ordered the "enemy," surprised and overwhelmed, to retire. Their cannon fired over their heads as the hostile infantry withdrew and, since their squadrons of aircraft had taken the air first, the retreat now had to break into a rout.

"We've more than offset the advantage they had over us," one of them said. "Because they marched so far yesterday, the fighting began early instead of in the afternoon."

"They cut us up pretty badly yesterday."

"We had to keep on the go clear up to evening."

"Well, what price their victory now?"

"Just look at them run. And all we've got to do today is play."

"Play? Where do you get that play stuff? We'll run till our tongues hang out."

"That's right. We haven't had a smell of it yet."

"We haven't the foggiest idea how things really

stand. It looks good for us right here, but that's no sign our boys aren't having a rough time of it somewhere else."

"Any way you take it the infantry's got to do all the work."

"Don't worry. The sooner we start the sooner we'll get the signal to quit."

"All right, if that's the way of it."

And so the soldiers went on talking.

The new day still kept its coolness. The sun was just rising and the soldiers were rested and cheerful. George marched along in the skirmish line, Renni at his left, and the three stretcher-bearers beside him.

Renni had had a drink of water and a few mouthfuls of good food and he danced about with a springy step, looking up joyfully at his master, who talked to him in a kindly tone all the time. George recalled happily how the captain had been worried because Renni was such a pup. He laughed.

"Well, that hard-boiled officer ought to have sense

enough to know he doesn't know anything." He thought of Vogg and how indifferent he could be to his line of talk now, after all that Renni had done. Let him just go on believing that George had whipped his dog.

The sun burned down hotter from the hazy sky. An oppressive sultriness lay over the land. Marching became a wearisome business. Hours passed. None of the enemy was in sight. They marched on. Somebody called out, "This is the play you were talking about." They marched on. Black clouds rolled up threateningly. When the storm broke with its first flash of lightning and peal of thunder, Renni pressed fearfully against his master. The roaring of man-made machines, a much more fearful racket than the storm, had made no impression on him, but the raging elements filled the brave dog with fear. With tail between his legs and a pleading look on his face he pressed closer and closer.

"What's the matter with you, fellow?" Renni jumped up on George, buried his head against his breast and seemed to beg, "Protect me." George pretended to be calm and cheerful and kept petting him, but he could not revive the dog's courage. The instant the thunder and lightning, the roaring of the winds, came to an end and the quick rain began to fall, Renni grew easy, though now and then he still cast an anxious glance at the sky.

For a little while the rain cooled the men off. Then they suffered again from the close, damp air. They felt the heat worse then ever. Suddenly they were fired at from both sides. They had fallen into an ambush and were being riddled. They had to fight now and they had their dander up. The mad burst of cannon fire began again, the chattering of machine guns, the howling of propellers, the rattle of musketry which sounded like banners cracking in the breeze. The men threw themselves on the wet, rain-soaked earth. Again Renni did exactly what was expected of him. He crouched down like the soldiers and crept along the ground sniffing in deep breaths. George had good reason to know that he was doing it all of his own accord.

Suddenly, without rising, with just a quick turn, Renni wriggled away. He was gone some time. Then, still crouching, he slipped up again and got George and the stretcher-bearers, who crept along after him on their bellies. A man had fallen into a deep ditch under his machine gun and could not move. They had a good deal of trouble setting him free and lifting the gun out. He seemed unharmed, only a little unsteady on his legs.

The firing raged on. The regiment had to use all its skill, resource and caution to escape from the ambush, but finally it succeeded. Renni sniffed the air. A second storm drew on. George was worried about the dog, but this time its only effect was to make him stick closer to his master. He continued to sniff the air all about. His ears pricked up sharply and he wagged his tail slowly but expectantly. All at once he leaped up and charged away. In a little while he crawled back and urged his master and the stretcher-bearers to come with him. He seemed so impatient that all four of them jumped to their feet and began to run after the flying dog. They gave no heed to the calls that followed them:

"Get down! Get down, you! Crawl!"

They pretended not to hear and in the crash of battle perhaps they did not. When the dog stopped, wagging his tail violently, his muzzle pointed straight down, the four shocked men found themselves standing over their major. He lay in a soft puddle. He must have fallen headlong over a slippery root and struck his head on a sharp stone. A major in the mud!

They wasted no time in thought. They turned the dazed man over, washed the blood from his cheek and nose, and tried to pick him up. He moaned and the pain brought him back to consciousness.

"I don't . . . know . . . what happened to me," he stammered, stupefied.

When they tried again a sharp groan burst from him.

"My ankle–I'm afraid it's broken."

"Let's hope it's only sprained, Major."

He smiled at George. "Oh, it's you," he said wearily. "And your dog found me?"

"Yes, sir. My Renni found you."

"A splendid animal, really a wonderful animal. . . . Who knows how long I've been lying here?"

"It can't have been long, sir. Not very long. Renni's been hunting all the time."

"A noble animal. That's the word for him–noble."

At last they got him up to level ground. He stifled his groans heroically.

"Get a stretcher," George ordered. Two of the bearers went off at a run. "Major, we'll have to carry you on a stretcher to the ambulance. You'd suffer too much if we tried it all the way on our shoulders."

"Thank you, thank you. But you'll stay with me?"

"At your orders, sir."

Again George washed his face, streaked with blood from a wound on the left cheekbone.

"Ah, that helps."

"How did this happen, Major?"

"Why, really, I don't know. Evidently I'm as dumb as any rookie. The first thing I knew I was lying there and it was all over. It must be that way when a man is shot down in war."

A distant bugle sang out. The call was repeated here and there, nearer and nearer. "The signal to cease operations for today," smiled George.

"No telling how long they'll cease for me. Beastly

luck!" The major felt round in his tunic for his cigarette case. George held a match for him. Renni had stretched out by the wounded man, smelled him over carefully and then in quiet confidence laid his head on his breast.

"How beautiful a dog's face can be," said the major, "and how he honours me. Yes, a man is downright honoured when an animal like that . . ." He broke off and turned to Renni. "Do you get the scent of my pup Tyras on me? Yes? Well, he can't do all the things you can, not by a long way. I've taught him only to shake hands. I didn't have to whip him to teach him that."

"I beg your pardon, sir, but my Renni's never been whipped. Never. Not once."

"Great! That's most unusual, and the kind of thing I like to hear. I hate to see animals beaten. Dogs, horses, cattle–it makes no difference. I hate it. How much honour and honesty are in a dog's face! Of course, I don't need to tell you that. But have you ever observed the high-strung courage in the eyes, the movements of a horse? The strong and gentle beauty of the eyes and heads of cattle?"

George would have liked to shake the major's hand, but discipline kept him from it. At that moment Renni sprang up unexpectedly and ran off as straight as a die.

"You'll excuse me, sir; I must follow the dog. The stretcher-bearers will be here straightway. If someone should be needing us, we can shorten his waiting and suffering by . . ."

"Go right ahead," cried the major.

George saw the stretcher-bearers coming up and signalled them to hurry. He took the third with him. This time it was only a soldier who had collapsed under the burden of his field equipment and the severe work of the day. They helped him to his feet. Embarrassed over his condition, he panted, "I'm a reservist."

"I too," thought George, but he said nothing.

The reservist went on, breathless, "I'm a government clerk. After an indoor life I can't stand this killing grind."

"You ought to report yourself exhausted and unfit for duty," advised the stretcher-bearer.

"That's what I'm going to do," the man said bitterly.

Then of a sudden he screamed, "Let me alone, you cur!" and kicked at the frightened, dodging Renni with his heavy boot.

"Say, you!" George blazed out at him. "Haven't you got any sense? That dog found you. Kick him, would you? Not while I'm about. Thank him."

"Thank him! Is that so? Well, thank you very kindly, Mr. Dog. The brute did his duty, and that's all there is to it."

"It's not everyone can say that for himself," George remarked dryly.

"You mean to compare me with that cur, Corporal?"

"No, I wouldn't insult the dog."

"You think I'll stand for it when he sticks his stinking snout in my hand? You think I won't kick him?"

George stood still. He ordered the stretcher-bearer: "Take this fellow in by yourself. If I go, I'll report his actions, and his insolence will be punished." He turned away with Renni, who did a joyful dance around him. He left plenty of room as he walked around the clerk and struck off through the woods.

"What do we care for trash like that, Renni? We don't care a rap, do we?"

A short, happy bark. Renni leaped up on his master and laid his forepaws on his shoulders so that George had to stop for a moment. He took Renni's head in his two hands. "You want to tell me I'm right? Clever of you, old man. We two . . . But come on, partner. We're both wet to the skin. Let's step along. Perhaps we'll get something hot to eat."

Renni trotted obediently at his master's left side, sniffing and from time to time laying his muzzle in George's hand. A short walk to a neat little town. Their quarters were with friendly people in a roomy old house. Many soldiers were there, and they gave Renni an enthusiastic greeting. They led him and his master to the kitchen, where they offered him the place of honour before the stove. Renni sat down, stared into the flames, dried his coat. After he had soaked up the comfortable waves of heat through his body, he got so hot that he panted and his tongue hung out. Meanwhile George stretched his wet clothes before the stove. Then they had a bite to eat.

"Does anyone know how the major's getting on?"

None had even heard of the accident.

The stretcher-bearer who had been left with the reservist came in to report. "That guy's a big fool. He laid down on me, said he wasn't going to walk another step. He bawled like a baby. Say, Corporal, don't you want to go to bed? You must be tired. There's a bed for you on the second floor."

"A bed?" George thanked him, laughing. "Just bring me a mattress here in front of the stove. We'll sleep like kings on it, Renni and I."

The soldiers laughed and dragged up a mattress. George stretched out. Renni stood before him, his tail a question mark.

"Why, of course you may, Renni. Just lie down beside me." Renni understood. He crept softly over, pressed close against George, and laid his muzzle on his shoulder. He sighed once, comfortably, before he went to sleep.

The other two stretcher-bearers came into the kitchen to report to George.

"Well, what is it?" George's tone was low, but Renni raised his head and pricked up his ears, wide awake.

"Everything's all right. The major's ankle is only sprained a little. He'll be dancing again in a week or so."

"That's fine," said George. "Where have they put him?"

"In the barracks–his own quarters."

Renni was again sleeping soundly by the time George told the stretcher-bearers to see about their food and a place to sleep. And George himself sank to sleep with a happy heart.

So ended the second day of the manœuvres.

Chapter XV

ON THE THIRD DAY REVEILLE sounded somewhat later than usual and they formed ranks more slowly.

"Today, we're the rear guard," the word went around.

"I don't understand that," one said.

"My dear friend," a high, squeaky voice put in, "what do you supes know about this battle anyway?"

"The main body of our army," declared a jolly bass,

"is fighting farther north. Any supe has sense enough to know that."

"We'll get the umpire's decision today," another ventured.

There was a general outburst of laughter. "Marvellous! Marvellous! Just think of that on the last day of manœuvres!"

"Toward noon the bugles will blow to cease operations," said a non-commissioned officer.

They laughed at him too for saying what they all knew, and a smart voice asked him earnestly, "Is that the order of the day, General? Then of course we'll just have to stop at noon. Won't that be awful?"

"Children," roared a giant infantryman, "children, perhaps we'll have no more fighting to do."

"Well, that won't hurt my feelings any," a pale lad said dryly.

From the distance came the roar of heavy artillery. Machine guns snapped viciously. They began to march in column formation. Renni walked along beside George in regulation step, his head lowered, his tail swinging half-sideways. There was no work for him to do yet. The farther forward they went the farther away the battle receded. From this they concluded that the "enemy" was retreating and that they were victorious. High spirits sparkled along the ranks. Here and there a song was started but the sharp command of "Silence!" ripped it to tatters. So they marched along talking in undertones. The blue sky called for good humour. The air had been cooled by yesterday's storm and there was not enough heat to be bothersome. Hour after hour they marched. At last, a forest. The command: "Form in skirmish lines! Guns ready! Fix bayonets!"

The formations began to break up and trickle into the woods. Then came the bugle calls, well known and long looked for, greeted with loud cries of joy, "The manœuvres are over!" "Cease operations!"

Guns, knapsacks, helmets with white bands lay all around them, tokens that a struggle had taken place here and the enemy been routed. A pause for rest. The big infantryman spoke up: "Didn't I tell you we wouldn't see any more fighting?"

"Yes, you old Napoleon, you military genius, you."

"Just look at Renni." Indeed it was wonderful to see him hurry along with his nose to the ground. He stopped unexpectedly, sniffed, and struck off on a different tack.

"He's lost the trail."

"Not on your life," declared George, never for a moment taking his eyes off the dog.

"But he doesn't know what to do. There's nothing for him to find now."

"You just wait and see," smiled George.

"Look here. The regiment that was driven out of this place certainly must have taken care of its own casualties."

At this moment Renni gave them the answer. He stopped beside a dark mass which gradually took human form. He sniffed at it, turned about, took up the trail by which he had come. On the way he stopped before another man who flung both arms around him and tried to help himself up. Renni shook him off and rushed toward George who was coming to meet him with his three helpers. Renni would not let them give first attention to the second man, as they started to do. He leaped away from him once and again till George grasped that he insisted they look first to that motionless body lying farther on.

Bending over the unconscious form, George said, "He's right. Wise Renni. This fellow is the worse case."

It was no easy matter to bring him back to his senses. Revived at last, he stammered out that he had either fallen or been knocked down, and who knows how many soldiers had tramped over him. On his uniform they could see the marks of hob nails. Two stretcher-bearers carried him away. Then George turned to the other soldier, who had his arms stretched out. He was conscious but said he had been knocked out for a long time and had not come to till the dog had touched him. He was in a pretty bad way after all. A motor cycle had run into him from behind and gone over him. He complained about his chest.

"We'll have to wait till the others come back," George said.

The man probably had some ribs broken but he waited patiently. Renni meanwhile had got a whiff of something not very clear to him. Uneasily he ran a few steps this way and that. He drew in deep breaths of air, testing it, and finally with sudden decision darted away. The stretcher-bearer growled. "Well, they've left us to do all their mopping up."

George looked for the dog, who was now out of sight. The two bearers came back. While they were laying the second man on their stretcher, Renni loped up, panting from excitement and a long, hard run.

"Follow me with the stretcher, when you're free," George commanded the bearers. "You never know how serious it may be." He turned to Renni, who had pawed at him eagerly. "Yes, yes. I'm coming." Renni pushed ahead so nervously, turned about so often to get George, it was plain he thought he was not coming fast enough. In the heart of a dense thicket a deep crack in the earth yawned so suddenly before them that George almost fell into it. Renni scooted down the steep slope on his hind quarters and George leaped after. He stared in horror at the soldier lying there, his face shattered and bloody, his helmet rolled to one side, his gun fallen from his bloody hand.

"He must be dead," said George to Renni, but Renni had another opinion. He wagged his tail violently.

George knelt down to listen at the naked breast and caught a feeble pulse that at times quickened feverishly. He nodded to his dog.

"You're right again. And you were right to make me hurry. For all that, I'm afraid we're too late and this boy will die on our hands before we can get him out."

But Renni swung his plume confidently while George talked. And while he talked George looked over the blood-stained hand, saw the danger instantly, got out a bandage, bound it tightly around the wrist, raised the arm up over the forehead and held it in place with a bandage about the armpit. The stream of life which at first trickled red through the bandage stopped running and began to form a protecting clot. George wiped the blood from the burnt face as best he could.

"How could this accident have happened? How could it have gone unnoted? Oh, perhaps the gun will explain things."

The lock was blown to bits, the magazine shattered by the exploding blank cartridges. Blank cartridges? Evidently, for there were no bullets about. The man must have plunged blindly along and fallen into this God-forsaken hole in the ground or been blown into it by the explosion. Perhaps . . . Perhaps. If he lived he could tell them all about it, or as much as he remembered. If not, then the experts in ballistics might throw light. Well, in any case the poor fellow must be got out of here in a hurry.

"Three men beside me will hardly be enough," George said to Renni. "Go, old friend, and fetch them."

Renni climbed to the top swiftly. George put his whistle to his lips and gave three shrill blasts. A number of soldiers hurrying up, called back and forth till they located the gorge. They stood at the edge, looking down horrified and offering all sorts of advice.

George called up to them, "We can't do anything

more for him till the stretcher gets here. Before it comes, get some strong ropes."

Several ran off for the ropes. The others discussed the accident.

"Here's another one they left behind."

"Maybe they didn't see him."

"Well, what about those two back there? Didn't they see them either?"

"Murderers! That's what they are."

"It's easy to say 'murderers,'" said George, "but after all they're our comrades, and they were retreating."

"Haven't they got any Red Cross dogs of their own?"

"Apparently not, or at least no good ones."

"Well then, who found this poor fellow?"

A number of voices called, "Why, Renni, of course."

"Good old Renni! You can always count on him."

Renni, leading the trio of stretcher-bearers, pressed through the groups and made ready to coast down again.

"Stay up there, old fellow," said George in a low voice. "You're not needed here and would just be in the way."

He lay down obediently and watched the stretcher-bearers carefully balance their slippery way down into the gulch. The soldiers patted him and he was friendly with them all but not too friendly.

George listened again at the breast of the wounded man. He was still unconscious. His heart was beating a little more calmly, but his brow was feverish and his breathing slow and irregular.

"If it's possible let's push the stretcher under him and save him the torture of being lifted up. And the risk. In the shape he is in it would be a ticklish business."

"Well, luckily, this stretcher hasn't any legs," said one of the bearers. "It's only a question whether the ground's soft enough to let us slip it under him."

"The ground down here is soaking wet," George assured him.

Deep silence prevailed while with George's help the bearers moved the canvas softly, carefully, inch by inch, under the wounded body. Once there was a momentary scare and a long pause. The wounded man had moaned softly.

"That's not a bad sign," said George in a hushed voice.

In silence the soldiers let down the ropes. The bearers fastened them around the four handles. Every care was taken to hold the stretcher level. When the motionless form reached the surface, a solemn voice said, "That was the exact opposite of a burial."

George looked to be sure that the wrist was no longer bleeding. Then he laid on the stretcher the gun, the shattered magazine, the helmet with the blood-sprinkled white band, and so let the three bearers carry their burden away. The men crowded excitedly about him.

"You've got to have something to eat at once."

"My dog must eat, of course, but I don't feel at all hungry."

"Hurry up. We've no time to lose."

"We're to march immediately."

"But, comrades, don't you understand that after a man has seen a thing like that he loses his appetite?"

"Aren't you a doctor?"

"A doctor? Why, take a look at me and you'll see I'm not. In civil life I'm a gardener."

"Well, anyway, a surgeon couldn't have done a better job of it."

"That's where you're wrong. Any doctor could have done better. All I'm doing is handling my dog."

"And no man could have done better than your Renni."

George laughed. "You're right there. But you don't go far enough. No human being in the world can do what a dog can."

Chapter XVI

AS SOON AS THE TROOPS BEGAN to move, the regimental band struck up a stirring march. The soldiers hummed the melody and swung along at a lively gait. George sang too, or hummed rather, and his pace quickened. He kept smiling down at the dog by his side while he put words to the music:

"What we have done was not so bad,

Old boy, old boy,

What we have done was not so bad. . ."

Renni looked up at him affectionately.

"Halt!" The command passed down the ranks. "Halt!" The music broke off suddenly. "What's the matter?"

Many men stepped out of rank to get a look up forward. At some distance houses were to be seen, and massed in front of them stood troops, troops, more troops. A part of the artillery, the tanks and machine guns, and even the field kitchens were lined up in front with the infantry massed behind them. The arrangement was more or less accidental.

"We're going to parade before our corps commanders."

"But with the order all backward."

"What do you mean, order? There's no order. Nothing but confusion."

"It makes no difference. Marching out in line after a manoeuvre isn't a parade anyhow."

"But we surely ought to have a parade."

"It would mean a bawling-out for a lot of the high-ups."

"Well, we won—that's what counts."

Slowly the planes in squadron formation roared

over their heads, the propellers humming in unison. Then came the metallic grinding of the tanks, the rumbling of the artillery, the rattling of the field kitchens. It took a long time. Renni lay down with his head on George's toes. Several of the soldiers stepped up with oak leaves in their hands.

"Renni's going to have a victory wreath."

Renni awoke with a start at the sound of his name and sat up on his hind quarters.

"Here we come to decorate you, Renni," the men said to him.

He pounded the ground with his tail in sign he understood they were speaking to him. While one wove the wreath the others addressed half-humorous words of praise to the dog, who kept wagging his tail more and more rapidly, looking first one and then another in the face. He seemed to smile. The soldier with the wreath drew nearer.

"Please don't, please don't," George begged them.

"Look there, Renni. Your master's jealous."

"Sure he is, Renni. He's envious of you."

"You see, Renni, that's the way people are. No matter how great a service a fellow does, they grudge him his reward."

"Oh well, then, let's put a wreath on the corporal, too."

"Sure, he's earned one as much as Renni."

"Help! Help!" cried George in mock fright.

They hung the wreath around the dog's neck. Renni shook himself violently three or four times trying to back out of his strange necklace, while the soldiers roared with laughter. Almost at once, the dog got the idea that the whole thing was a joke. With his head down between his paws he dared them to catch him; then he started tearing around in short circles. The wreath tickled him. Struggling to get rid of it he indulged in the wildest leaps and plunges, and danced about on his hind feet as if he were crazy.

"It looks wonderful on you," they called to him. "You're going to make a hit, Renni."

"They'll all think you belong to the circus."

Renni slowed down, almost stopped, trying first with

his front feet and then with his hind legs to get through his collar of prickly leaves. He kept at it till at last the wreath torn to pieces, fell from him. He went mildly mad over this achievement, leaped up on his master, resumed his breathless running around in circles.

All at once the band up front blazed away with a fanfare.

"Here," called George in a low voice. As Renni instantly took his safe place by his left side, he snapped the leash into his collar. They walked along in step to the music. George said, "I'd have set you free from that stuff, partner."

The dog looked up at him with such love and confidence that it seemed he must have understood him word for word.

The soldiers stepped along more briskly. The heavy drums quickened the time. They marched into a large square surrounded by tall houses with flags at every window.

George saw the general standing alone in front of a group of officers, the colonel a half-pace to the rear with gleaming sabre in his hand. As the officers passed they gave the salute, and the general returned it. Rank and file saluted by pulling briskly at the gun straps and turning their heads sharply to the right where the corps commander stood. In the rear of the battalion, George, who had no gun, kept his right hand at his visor as they passed by. Suddenly he saw the general point at him questioningly. The colonel nodded, and then he realised that the general was smiling and waving to him. The general waving to him! An agony of pride went over him. He turned red as fire. When he had got safely past the reviewing stand and into the school yard where they were to camp for the night, he whispered to Renni, "That was meant for you."

At the dog's look of love he bent down and put his arms about him. Hardly had he entered the room which he was to share with six first-aid men, among them Sergeant-Major Nickel, hardly had he and Nickel shaken hands and old Hector and young Renni exchanged greetings, when the adjutant appeared with word for George to report to the colonel. In a sort of daze, he asked Nickel, "May I leave Renni with you?" But the adjutant said gruffly, "Bring your dog, of course."

When they reached the gymnasium George walked stiffly toward the colonel, who left the group of officers and came to meet him. He reported, "At your orders, sir."

The colonel shook hands with him, a distinction so rare it attracted attention on all sides. George could not stop a deep blush from spreading over his face. They liked him the better for it.

"The regiment may well be proud of you, Corporal." The colonel spoke in a loud voice. He bent over the dog so George might have time to recover from his embarrassment.

"Well, you're a fine dog, Renni. You've done a great deal, a very great deal. How shall we reward you?"

Renni's tail whirled violently at the caress and he acted as though he were going to put his forepaws on the colonel's breast. George held him back on the leash.

"Let him alone, Corporal. Let him alone. A dog like that doesn't know distinctions of rank, do you, Renni?"

The dog reached out one fore foot and pawed softly at the colonel who took it in his hand and went on speaking.

"We can congratulate ourselves that there's no such thing as rank with you. Officers and men, we're all just friends you want to help. So it is a real pleasure to me to carry out the general's instructions, Renni, and to give you his warmest commendation." He smiled. "And you, too, Corporal. You see, everyone knows your dog's name. He's famous."

And with that he freed Renni's foot. The dog must have been impressed by his solemn but cordial words. By the gentle waving of his tail he gave the proceeding his tacit approval.

"To that I wish to add my personal thanks and the praise and gratitude of all the officers, and of the rank and file," the colonel concluded. George was on the point of retiring but he called him back.

"You'rc a corporal in the reserve?"

"Yes, Colonel."

"Your profession in civil life?"

"A gardener, Colonel."

"You may take the train home. The adjutant will write your pass for you."

George saluted. "Thank you, sir." He hesitated, for he was much touched. "If the Colonel will permit I'd like to ask permission to remain with my regiment till the end."

"Good. That's exactly what I'd have expected from a man like you. Use your Renni after his desert and he'll 'scape whipping. Good-bye."

George, who did not catch the reference to *Hamlet*, would have liked to assure the colonel that he had never struck Renni, but force of discipline curbed the impulse. He saluted and withdrew.

On the way back to his room he might have shouted for joy, but indeed his happiness was so deep and serious it kept him quiet. When Sergeant-Major Nickel inquired how things had gone, George only told him in a few words that the general had praised his dog's services. Then he excused himself on the score of weariness and went to bed. But he lay awake a long time beside the sleeping dog, stroking his head, his neck, his back.

• • •

Early in the morning the regiment was under way, for they wanted to take advantage of the early morning hours before the heat became oppressive. George would have liked to see the major again but was not given time. It wasn't for lack of courage. He wouldn't now have been afraid to approach the major's bed. After the distinction he had received, it would not have seemed presumptuous or a bid for praise.

To the accompaniment of regimental music they marched half the forenoon, stopped for a few hours' rest, marched on until it grew dark. All in the best of spirits. They were getting plenty to eat and their quarters for the night were comfortable if simple. There was no work for Renni. The men who dropped out from sore feet or sickness did not have to be hunted up. They merely stepped out of the line, and the Medical Corps took care of them. Several times George met Nickel, and Renni met Hector.

"Your dog," said Nickel, "is an exception to all rules. You certainly have a right to be proud of his training."

It developed that Hector too was a product of Vogg's

kennels. Nickel had a small soap factory in the same town where George had his field and garden. His liking for dogs and his helpful attitude had afforded him the chance for this Red Cross work.

"That way I've escaped the nuisance of being just a high private in the rear rank," he said good-naturedly. "Of course, military service is important. Of course. In case of attack we can't be defenceless. But it's just as important that . . . You know what I mean. Well, then, in case of need there must be men who can do what has to be done."

They talked of Vogg. George told how he had been insulted by him without cause. Nickel took up the cudgels for the old breeder.

"Forget it, my friend, forget it. Vogg knows well enough you're not the man to beat a dog. He knows it all right. He just has these spells when his temper gets poisonous and then he acts crazy. He starts abusing people right and left. He knows better. He's just a peculiar kind of fanatic. Outside that he's the best man on earth."

It took them four days to march back to the point where the battalion had assembled, George's home town. The staff officer in the Medical Corps who had snarled at him when they started off called him over with a brief nod.

"Just want to tell you," he growled, "I was mistaken. Your dog went far beyond my expectations."

Again he took hold of Renni's leash, pulled him gently over, bent down, patted his back in friendly fashion. "Now, now, old boy. Nobody ever learns everything. So I owe you this much of an apology."

"Will the Captain permit me a word?" asked George, hand at visor.

The answer was a sharp command, "Speak up! What is it?"

"I should like to beg the Captain's pardon. . . ."

"Pardon? What for?"

"For my attitude."

Just the shimmer of a smile went over the officer's stern features. "I don't know what you're talking about. Forget it! Dismissed!"

• • •

George was home again at last. He opened the garden gate, and Renni charged through, almost upsetting the welcoming household. His greeting was not short of violent for everyone except Ludmilla and Vassili. Not till Kitty came out of the house, leaped onto Renni's neck, and both of them rolled playfully on the ground, was George free to go in and speak to them all.

"It worked beautifully, Mother. Beautifully."

"I was sure it would, son."

"Where are Bettina and Vladimir?"

"They're just now burying old Nemo. The poor thing died this morning."

"Do you see?" smiled Ludmilla, offering George her hand; "if you had just followed my advice and killed him . . ."

Vassili finished in his slow, solemn tones, "The poor beast would have been spared a great deal of suffering."

"He didn't suffer at all," interrupted Mitya.

Mother Marie said quietly, "Dying is a holy thing. Nobody has the right to take it on himself to cut short the life of any creature that loves and trusts him, or to fix the hour of death."

Ludmilla looked helplessly around until Vassili boomed, "An unsolved problem!"

"Anyhow, it's a satisfaction to me that I could give him a few weeks of quiet life," said George.

Tanya came to his aid energetically. "People who kill an old dog or a sick cat make themselves believe it's out of pure sympathy. But they must know that they're really doing it just for their own comfort."

Bettina and Vladimir came in from their sad task. Vladimir said quietly, "We buried him under the big cherry tree. It was touching how nice he looked, good old Nemo."

Bettina was silent. She petted Renni, who pressed close against her.

"Tell us about it, George," urged Vladimir.

"Yes, do," begged Bettina.

Renni went over to Tanya with a low growl of content.

She pushed him down. "Quiet now. We're going to talk about you."

The dog looked at her curiously, his ears pricked up.

"Let's drink our tea first," Ludmilla demanded.

"We can do both," decided Mother Marie: "drink and listen."

"You always find the best way out," Ludmilla said affectionately. She had begun to fear she might have to wait for her beloved tea.

So George told all that had happened.

Renni, hearing his name frequently, got up, went cautiously over to his master, sat down between his knees and looked up into his face, turning his head to one side and swinging his tail slowly as if he would testify to all the truth of the simple story.

PART III

Chapter XVII

RENNI WAS AT A LOSS IN THE peaceful days which followed. There was nothing to do, none to hunt for, no marching, no sleeping at night before the stove by his master's side. He missed all that, and he missed the noisy, friendly soldiers, who praised him so and gave him so much credit. While he had been away at manœuvres his ambition had awakened. It was as innocent as it was eager, but it might easily have been mistaken for conceit. He had quickly grown used to doing important things, had come to expect that a man here and there would have need of him, and he liked being the centre of interest and attraction. Now he found himself forced to be idle. Nothing was asked of him now. He did not know what to do with himself.

The first night he had jumped into bed with George; he thought that his sleeping place was still close beside his master. Kitty, out in the hallway, called him, mewing pitifully.

George raised up. "No, old man. The manœuvres are over. Here at home we'll do things the old way. Don't you hear Kitty asking for you?"

And with that he ordered the crestfallen dog out of the bed, and showed him his proper place on the mattress. Renni, obedient as usual, did what was expected of him, though he was not a little disappointed. But Kitty made things easier for him. She welcomed her bedfellow warmly and affectionately, pressed against his side and purred loudly. She had had to do without him for two weeks.

George stuck close to home for the first few days,

partly because he felt the need of a good rest, partly because his garden and fields needed him badly. Renni followed him step by step, looking at him all the time as if he were eagerly waiting for something. He watched every movement, and his eyes said plainly, "When are you going to need me again?"

George tried to pacify him. "Yes, yes, you're a fine fellow. You don't have to work and worry any more. Take a good long rest and be happy."

His master's kind words hardly measured up to the praises they had given him away from home. Renni did not want to rest, he did not need to, and his eagerness to be doing something kept him unsatisfied.

They began their walks in the forest again. Just as soon as they left the house Renni would be as gay as he could be. Out here in the woods, he thought, he'd be needed again. There would be men to look for, find, and help. He trotted along, with his muzzle at his master's left knee and often in George's hand. But he would run repeatedly to the edge of the bushes, sniff the air with nose held high, ears pricked up, and tail waving energetically. Then in disgust he would turn back to the road.

"What do you want?" George would respond to his mute but insistent questioning. "There's nothing there." Renni took his word for it, but still kept looking for something. He would come back home in deep dejection, his ears close against his head, his tail hanging slack. Every walk in the woods began full of happy hope and readiness for service. But, after all the sniffing and trailing, every walk came to futile and disappointed end.

Once George could not resist Renni's impatient desire to do something, and he started out through the thickets. The dog ran ahead, thoroughly in his element. Every moment he would stop, listen, test the air, thinking, "Now . . . now . . ."

George meant well but must have gone about it the wrong way. Renni came out of the bushes sad, almost heartbroken. In the road he sat down on his hind quarters, his head hanging. He was in despair. The look he gave George seemed to say, "Does no one need me any more?"

George stroked his melancholy face. "Next year, Renni, next year . . . at manœuvres . . ."

Ah, next year things were to be far more serious, nothing like the harmless play-war of the manœuvres. But no one had an inkling of that yet–certainly no one among the peaceful mass of common people.

Mother Marie, when George spoke to her about Renni, said, "He'll quiet down after a bit."

Bettina declared emphatically, "If Renni hasn't anything to do for too long a time, he'll forget everything!"

George replied, laughing, "Forget? That dog forget? To be helpful is in his blood. He won't forget anything."

Bettina shrugged her shoulders. "A year's a long time, and it will be a year before the next manœuvres."

Her words made George thoughtful. He told Vladimir and Tanya about it. Tanya said, "Don't worry. You don't forget how to ride a bicycle or a horse, do you? Do you think you would forget how to read and write even if you didn't read or write anything for years?"

But Vladimir grinned. "Ever know a dog that could ride a bicycle? Or a dog that could read and write? Well, then! After all a dog is a dog, not a person. I'd be in favour of starting practice again with Renni. Bettina's right."

"Of course," Tanya nodded. "Your Bettina's always right."

"So she is." Vladimir's grin spread wide.

"*Your* Bettina?" asked George, taken aback. "So that's the way of it?"

"Oh, nonsense!" Vladimir grew red and left the room.

Now that his eyes were opened, George noticed that Vladimir was always around Bettina wherever she worked, even in the kitchen; and that she showed a fondness for his company, and seemed especially to like being alone with him.

George made no comment. He had nothing against it, only he thought now and then of the objections that Vladimir's parents were bound to raise. But somehow George did not realise how much of the time he himself kept near Tanya, how pleasant the work was when she helped him, and how anxious she was to have Renni's good will.

He decided to resume practicing with Renni and asked Kolya and Mitya to be wounded men again. When they fixed on a day, Tanya asked unexpectedly, "May I go to the forest with you?" She blushed prettily as she said it.

"Why, of course," George answered quickly and gladly. "I was just thinking of asking you."

Kolya and Mitya suppressed a laugh. Vladimir asked, "Want to play wounded?"

"I'd like to," replied Tanya seriously.

They went out to another forest, one where they had never been before. As he saw them start together, Renni guessed instantly what was afoot. He marched along beside George, as he was supposed to, for only a little way. Then he broke out in wild leaps around them, darted first to one side and then to the other, rolled in the grass, and carried on all manner of foolishness.

"Here you, what about discipline?" George called Renni and snapped the leash to his collar. The dog crept along, quite crestfallen. When Kolya and later Mitya turned aside into the woods, he sent a keen glance after them. And when Tanya vanished, he lifted his head, pricked up his ears, and waved his tail with joy. Playfully he found them all–Tanya first, with special delight. No matter how desperately they pretended to need help, he was not to be fooled. He pushed his muzzle gaily against their hips and shoulders, washed their faces with his tongue and would not give up till they admitted they were in perfect health.

Renni had mastered his job and carried it out in the easiest possible way. Once he had found them he was through, and with such good friends as Kolya, Mitya and Tanya, especially Tanya, he felt it was time for a romp. He had been through serious trouble, real duties, bloody wounds. He knew the difference between actual need of help and this game his friends wanted to play.

Twice more he plunged from the road into the thickets.

The first time George and the others heard a woman scream and children crying near by. Renni had run onto a mother having a picnic in the woods with her family. He came back with his tail between his legs.

The second time they heard a roar followed by a man's angry curses. He had been taking a nap and the dog had woken him up. Renni was utterly downcast, his eyes full of trouble, after his second failure to be useful.

"This is going to ruin him," said Tanya as they started home.

In a discouraged tone George said, "I just don't know what to do."

But Nickel, the soap-maker, solved the problem when he came with his dog Hector to pay a visit. Everyone liked Nickel, and soon he was everyone's good friend. Mother Marie especially smiled at him and listened to him with approval, for not only had Hector exchanged cordial greetings with Renni, but he had spoken very politely to her beloved Kitty, too.

Kitty lay down on her back between the two dogs, shared her graceful, coquettish slaps with them both, and purred loudly and happily.

Mother Marie and the others were frightened when Hector took Kitty's head in his powerful jaws, so that it was quite out of sight and seemed in a fair way to be crushed to bits. But Kitty herself did not seem at all worried; she clawed playfully at Hector and then let him wash her face, a task he performed with gravity and care.

"He won't hurt her," Nickel assured them. "He always does my cats that way. A dog makes up these little tricks on his own."

Mother Marie hid Kitty in her protecting arms; but in a moment the kitten wanted to get down to Hector again. She pressed close to his side, bracing her feet against Renni's breast.

When George asked his advice, Nickel laughed good-humouredly. "Why worry yourself and your dog? You'll only confuse him. Either a dog has it in him or he hasn't. Well, Renni has already showed that he has it all right! He won't ever forget any of it, lose any of it, not his whole life long. Look at my Hector. He's served in six manœuvres, six different years. All the time in between I've just let him play around and loaf as much as he pleased. And every year when the manœuvres begin, he acts as if he'd been in service no longer ago than yesterday!"

"That's just what I said," said Bettina smoothly, though, to be sure, she had said just the opposite. George was very much relieved.

With just the faintest trace of his grin Vladimir said, "Bettina's the cleverest person I know."

Nickel looked at them in some surprise, but heedless of Vladimir's and Bettina's embarrassment, he turned to George. "I'm really here because Vogg sent me."

George felt jolted, but quickly pulled himself up and said carelessly, "He did? What does he want with me?"

"He sends you his regards and wants you to bring Renni to see him."

"Well, he'll wait a long time."

"Come now, don't be hard on him. He's an old man."

"Does he expect me to swallow his insults and come running the minute he waves his hand? Not if I know myself!"

"He's an old man . . ."

"We all get to be old men, if we don't die first. It's no particular credit to him, and it gives him no rights at all."

"You ought to be grateful to him . . ."

George started up, then bethought himself, and said coldly, "I owe him nothing! I had the highest respect and regard for him. I proved it over and over. But when he accused me of lying . . . all that was wiped out. Everything. Gratitude, respect, everything! We're even, Vogg and I!"

"I'd never have thought you'd hold a grudge," Nickel said.

"Neither would I," said Mother Marie quietly.

The others too were surprised at George's refusal. He defended himself. "You're wrong. If I nursed a grudge, I'd be trying to think up ways to get even with die old man, wouldn't I? Well, I don't dream of it." He asked his friends, "Have you ever seen me do anything low or mean? He said right to my face that he wouldn't believe me on oath! That's enough for me! And you"–George looked at Nickel–"would you look up a man again after he'd told you to go hang yourself?"

Nickel answered after a pause, "He's sorry now."

George shrugged his shoulders. "A bit late!"

Chapter XVIII

WEEKS PASSED. ONCE MORE the Russians were at Mother Marie's tea table. She and George had been to the Safonoffs' once or twice, but as Bettina was never invited, they did not go any more. The old innocent happy friendship had disappeared. Vladimir, who bore the brunt, seemed changed. His face had taken on a serious and sometimes a sad expression, and he had stopped his melodious whistling.

This afternoon at George's Ludmilla was free with her bitter remarks. Her smile, so charming and appealing, gave way to a tight, thin-lipped sneer. Once she said abruptly, "Back in Russia the servants never sat down at table with the people of the house."

Without a word Bettina rose and left the room. Tanya followed her instantly, and Renni too slipped out. The others sat there speechless. George's anger boiled over. Vassili, visibly embarrassed, boomed solemnly, "You ought not to have said that, Millie."

But Ludmilla went on: "You, George, you are to blame for this. We have you to thank for this . . . this person. If you hadn't brought the little flirt to your house, she'd never have had the chance to take my son in!"

Vladimir hid his face in his hands. Before Mother Marie or anyone else could utter a word George snapped out, "I don't mean to argue with you! You're always right about everything! As far as I'm concerned you can think what you please. But I don't see why you keep on coming to our house. And I certainly won't let you insult anyone in it!"

Before he finished Vassili was on his feet. "Let us go, Millie." His voice was trembling. Ludmilla, pale, scared, tried to smile, to stammer an apology, but Vassili roared out, "Do you hear me! It is my wish that we go!"

He mastered his feelings, bowed low and ceremoniously, and stood aside to let Ludmilla pass out before him. She hesitated, gathered herself together from her worry and embarrassment, turned suddenly, strode hurriedly out as if in flight, and was weeping helplessly when she left the room.

For a moment Kolya and Mitya sat in petrified silence, then they followed their parents.

"You were too hard on her. I feel sorry for the silly little thing," said Mother Marie. "Did you see the tears running down her cheeks, big bright round tears? She was just like a child, like a little six-year-old girl. And she is a child, too. You shouldn't be so hard on her."

"The way she acted was unbearable," George growled. He was already half-sorry he had gone so far.

"Well, let's say a spoiled child, but she's certainly a child," smiled Mother Marie.

They both looked at Vladimir, who still sat cowering in his seat. Suddenly he sprang up, stood there for a moment, pale as a sheet, and then, painfully and slowly, forced out the words, "I . . . am . . . staying!"

Renni charged in, leaped up on George, on Mother Marie, on Vladimir, swung his tail like a swift pendulum, and repeated his attack as if he wanted to calm down the excitement and put cheerfulness in its place.

Tanya appeared, bringing Bettina with her. "Well . . ." She hesitated. "Are . . . are they all gone?" Mother Marie told what had happened.

"Oh, that won't hurt Mama in the least," Tanya said with great serenity. "If Papa hadn't been here she'd have asked everyone's pardon. Mama's good at heart. Only she hadn't any bringing up. Papa spoils her, pets her all the time and keeps her believing she can do whatever she pleases."

George confessed that he felt bad about it. "After all, she was our guest."

"Well, suppose she was! She broke all the laws of hospitality, ten times over!" Tanya argued. "Don't be sorry for anything, my friend! Regret is a sign of weakness. If you go around regretting your actions, you'll take all the vigour and freshness out of them. You'll just dry up." Her dark eyes were blazing.

"Well, sometimes the moment gets the better of you, and you forget yourself," said George.

"You must stand up for what you do even then," Tanya insisted.

"If you carry that argument far enough, you'll find excuse for criminals," said Mother Marie.

"What I'm saying," Tanya declared, "is true only of good people who are incapable of doing wrong. Criminals . . . there are criminals who are always repenting, the weak, addlepated creatures. They've fallen into a life of crime without intending to, and they go around whining. And then there are others who are criminals by instinct, by their own inner nature. They never regret anything! They're strong! And they should be put where they can do no harm!" She turned to Vladimir, who still sat there in silence, and ran her hand tenderly over his hair. "Poor brother!"

He hurried from the room. Tanya looked after him. "He always runs away. He acts as if he were afraid of himself. And yet he's got a strong will and, when the time comes, he'll stand up to anything or anybody!"

"I'm going with Vladimir. We didn't get our work finished," said Bettina in a hard tone and, as she left the room, she closed the door with a bang.

Renni had listened closely to the whole conversation, looking each one in the eye as he spoke, and had tried to draw attention to himself by friendly gestures. Finally he had stretched out, acting a bit timid and showing plainly that he understood how tense everyone was.

Now, as George and Tanya started for the fields, he joined them, quite happy.

Two, three weeks went by. Renni went out to the forest with George every day. He was especially happy when Tanya went along, and if Vladimir and Bettina joined the party, his joy knew no bounds. He would run from one couple to the other, leaping and dancing. He had entirely got over regretting the manœuvres, the feeling that he was out of a job. He was free, he was in vacation mood, he had nothing in the world to do but enjoy life.

Without mentioning it to anyone, George went to call on Ludmilla. He was received very stiffly. "I am astonished. . . ." Vassily began after a curt bow.

"You . . . you come to our house . . . ?" Ludmilla asked sharply.

George said frankly, "I came to see both of you but you particularly, Madame. Won't you please forgive me for my rudeness? Forgive me, I beg you most sincerely."

Ludmilla's eyes filled at once with big round tears.

"You ought to have come sooner. You ought to have come immediately," said Vassili stiffly.

Ludmilla interrupted him. "But . . . but . . . dear friend George . . . how nice of you to come!" She turned on her husband. "What do you mean, sooner? Why sooner? If he had come sooner we would still have been angry at him. Now . . . is the time . . . dear, dear George." In her gush of emotion her words choked her and then fell over one another and she gave him no chance to speak. "I'm the one who should be begging your pardon . . . I . . . it was dreadful of me. I'm a wicked, wicked woman."

"No," declared George, "you're charming. You have a magic way about you! We all miss you so."

Laughing and weeping at the same time, Ludmilla cried, "Do you hear, darling? Do you hear?"

The solemn "Certainly I hear, Millie!" which Vassili murmured softly was lost in Ludmilla's torrent of words. "They miss me, Vassili! They miss us! But we miss you too, don't we, Vassili? And we've longed for you, for all of you. Oh, my dear, darling George, it was so lovely when we all used to have tea together at your house! It warmed the soul. When we quarrelled, we felt as if we had been banished, exiled a second time, we poor people who have no country left to us." Again her eyes filled with those big bright tears.

"Shall we forget it all and bury it forever?" suggested George. "If you can, I'm sure Mother and I can."

"Buried and forgotten!" Ludmilla cried.

She leaned over to George, threw an arm about his neck and kissed him on both cheeks.

Vassili said very gravely, "I cannot forget. . . . But as for forgiving . . ." He offered his hand and George took it.

"Holy Virgin of Kazan!" Ludmilla moaned suddenly. "We'll never get to come and see you again! I insulted Miss Bettina . . . I insulted her so terribly."

"Don't worry," George comforted her. "Bettina understands that you're against her."

"Did she say so?"

"Not a word. She never says anything," George admitted. "She'll be as friendly and kind as ever."

Ludmilla seemed convinced. "What a good girl! It's hard to believe! Just a girl of the common people, not pretty, but so good-hearted!"

Surprisingly Vassili said, with slow significance, "She is a noble woman."

When George reached home he started right in to give them the story.

"It's a relief to me on your account," Mother Marie said to him. "It worried me that you were so rude to the poor lady. It didn't seem like you."

"Well, I was glad to find out that George had the nerve to speak up to her. As a general rule he's far too easy going," was Tanya's opinion. She added, "My parents must have been very pleased. They've known all along that Mama deserved a calling down, but they never will admit how much they've missed coming here."

"Oh, yes indeed; they expressly said so," said George.

"Well, what do you know about that!" said Tanya.

Bettina and Vladimir were silent.

Right then Mitya and Kolya came in and were greeted noisily by Renni. It was as though they had been there no longer ago than yesterday, instead of weeks having passed. They played with the dog and teased the kitten without the slightest embarrassment.

Only, as they started to leave, plump Mitya took George's hand. "I'm so glad all that rot is over."

Big, lumbering Kolya, who was petting Renni, was more sceptical. "Mama will break out somewhere else. Just give her time. You can depend on it."

After a few days the old couple came over. They tried to act as if nothing had happened, but their stiffness was very marked. Vassili bowed lower than ever from the hips. It was quite a while before he seemed at ease. Ludmilla smiled her charming smile, though her eyes filled with tears when she threw her arms about Mother Marie.

She was wearing gloves and so could venture to pet Renni. "There you are, you good old dog." It sounded like the condescension of a queen.

But Renni had no relish for such favours. He looked around in astonishment, wagged his tail a little, very politely, and got away from Ludmilla as quickly as he could.

But there was no graciousness for Bettina. She was greeted with a slight nod only, and after that neither of them looked her way once. Vassili seemed to have forgotten he had called her a noble woman.

Still everything went off smoothly enough. The Safonoffs began coming over for tea almost every day. And as it happened they were there when Vogg came in unexpectedly.

"Why didn't you come to see me?" he snorted at

George. "I sent word to you, didn't I? Or hasn't Nickel been here?"

"Why don't you speak to these guests?" asked George.

Vogg looked at Vassili and Ludmilla contemptuously. "Those are the people who wanted to buy a whole pack of dogs to keep tied up. . . . Oh yes, I know them."

"We can dispense with this gentleman's courtesies," Vassili declared with every show of dignity and began to move towards the door.

Old Vogg stepped up to Mother Marie. "You're the mother, eh?" He shook her hand. "You have a fine son."

Just then Renni ran in between his legs and the eager swinging of the dog's tail almost upset him.

"Yes, you're friendly with me, aren't you?" Vogg patted him on the neck, took him by the muzzle and turned his face up to look in his eyes. "You don't get insulted, do you? You know what I mean, eh? You're a dog, and that's why we two get along so well. Go tell your master to come into another room with me or out in the garden, even if it is raining. How about it?"

The cat gave a leap and landed on his shoulder, stuck

her head up against his chin and purred loudly. He laughed, reached out for her gently and held her against his breast. "Well, animals are nice to me, anyhow."

"Oh, come on," George said. And the two, followed by Renni, went out into the hall. Then Vogg turned Kitty loose and spoke to George. "You wouldn't get off your perch and come to see me, eh?"

"I didn't begin the quarrel, Mr. Vogg. I never start fights, but I never make up, either."

"Why not, you hard-hearted villain?"

"Because . . . I can't get over a breach of friendship . . . that's why."

"I am an old man. You ought to have thought about that. But anyway," Vogg spoke more eagerly, "what's the use of talking about what might have been. I'm here now. I was unjust and it's worried me for a long time, even before Nickel told me . . . But don't let's act like men! Let's learn from the dogs! Let's not bear grudges."

He put out his hand and George took it. "Dogs, Mr. Vogg, note and remember everything we do to them. The good as well as the bad."

"Let that go for me." Vogg sat down on the floor and put both arms about Renni. The dog freed himself and tore around the hall. Kitty chased after him, graceful and dainty. It ended with all three–Renni, Kitty and Vogg–rolling together on the floor. George looked on in much better humour. Nothing more was said. Only, as he started to leave, Vogg, who had resumed his gruff, curt way of speaking, said, "Give my regards to your mother."

Chapter XIX

AUTUMN SOON TURNED TO winter, with pouring rains, violent winds, piercing cold. They sat comfortably in the living-room or did what there was to do in the house, packing potatoes and other vegetables away in the storeroom to keep them from freezing. When the boy Rurpert Fifer reported for work Mother Marie welcomed him warmly. His excessive enthusiasm for Renni ought to have been enough in itself to put them on their guard. He told how the dog had found him and saved his life, and adorned the tale with most fantastic details. Since there was no other work to be done George set him to chopping wood, but Rupert was slow about it and soon showed himself a lazy rascal. Nobody in the house could really like him, though all had been more than willing at first. Even Renni seemed to feel something in the fellow that kept him from his usual cheerful confidence; he was polite but reserved.

For the time being, they had little time to think of Rupert, for in George's house, as all over the country, political affairs had begun to attract an attention which they had never before aroused. This interest grew and grew, and the less they understood the political situation, the more violently they all debated it.

Vassili expressed himself very gravely. "It is to be hoped that you will remain at peace. It does not concern me, of course. Thank God, I had my war experience years ago and lived through it. I can tell you it would be a disaster."

Alarmed and serious, Ludmilla said, "War is a great disaster. There is no greater." She sighed deeply and made the sign of the cross.

George said, easily, "I know nothing at all about these things. Possibly for that very reason I don't see any danger."

Vladimir responded gloomily, "Yes, that's exactly why you don't see the danger." He was scanning the newspapers day by day.

And the language of the papers became more and more violent. Rumours fluttered through the air like moths, and from them all the only possible conclusion was that harmony and good will were hopelessly shattered.

The papers of the neighbouring country were no less inflamed.

"There's poison in their speech," wailed Mother Marie, who got her information from Vladimir.

George had apparently no interest in it all. "Just talk," he said, and he played with Renni or went out with him for a walk in the forest that now lay sleeping under its blanket of snow.

Renni loved the snow. He swallowed great mouthfuls of it, dived into it, scattering flakes in every direction, wallowed and buried himself so deep that he came out all crusted over with ice and snow and scarcely recognisable. Then he would shake himself wildly and George would have a task to get him brushed off clean.

Christmas was drawing near, but a burden of fear lay on all the people–on the working men, on the middle classes, and even on the rich. Many of the well-to-do deposited their money and valuables in foreign lands and exchanged their securities for foreign paper; and this made the national bonds fall disastrously. The palaces in the capital stood empty, guarded only by a few servants, while the families spent the winter at their castles in the country.

Business at Christmas time was poorer than it had been for years. Many factories closed down, so that the labourers were soon going hungry and began to complain bitterly. The government took a hand. A law was passed which set severe penalties for sending money out of the country, and another law which ordered businesses either to open their doors or be confiscated. The whole world was in a state of feverish excitement.

As the cost of food soared to fantastic heights the government fixed maximum prices. Then many important articles of food disappeared from the market and people took to buying and selling them secretly.

The whole huge, intricate and complicated machinery of living together, which as a rule runs so smoothly and steadily, now began to slow down. It threatened to become clogged in the mass of conflicting interests, and to stop altogether. The lessons of the World War called forth one emergency measure after another. But there was no severe distress yet.

George spoke in bitter terms of the rich who fled the country. Not till now was his interest in public affairs awakened. He was firmly convinced that his own nation was entirely in the right, but he knew very little about the points of difference and still could not believe that war was drawing near.

"You do not understand these people," Vassili said to him when George stormed against the rich who had emigrated. "You judge them too harshly, my friend." Vassili's solemn tone carried a trace of hurt feelings.

"You can't be too harsh!" cried George. "These people got wealthy here and now in its hour of need they desert the land that gave them their money. At the very first hint of danger! That's worse than cowardice. It's the blackest ingratitude, the lowest form of selfishness. It's treason!"

"I suppose you don't realise that your words might apply to us." Ludmilla smiled. "We would be beggars this minute if we had not left our country at the right time."

"That is so, precisely so," Vassili affirmed.

"But," said George, "your case is different, quite different. You were in a country in revolution. You saw the coming of the volcanic eruption in time. No revolution is to be feared here. Or are we on a sinking ship; that the rats are in such a hurry to get away?"

"Let's think about that," boomed Vassili. "Rats are clever animals. When they leave it is not a question of *possible* danger. You can be sure that *real* danger is very near at hand. Rats know more than you and I."

Ludmilla made the sign of the cross. "Perhaps we

ought to leave too. Maybe we should go south."

"There is still plenty of time for that, Millie," said Vassili. "We shall have to think it over a little."

"I'm going to stay here no matter what happens," Tanya declared.

Vladimir felt that same way about it. "I am not going to stir from this spot."

"Suit yourselves," said Vassili with ill humour.

And Ludmilla simpered, "Our other children will be only too happy to go with us."

From that day on George believed in the war.

Just before Christmas things came to a head with Rupert Fifer. George found the woodshed door standing open one day and heard Kitty crying and Renni growling inside. Then came an agonised howl. George alarmed, rushed in. Renni crept past him, crouching to the floor. Kitty, her back arched and her fur on end, stood on a high rick. As soon as she caught sight of George she made a leap for his breast as though to seek protection.

"What's going on here?" asked George.

Rupert shrugged his shoulders. "Nothing."

"You haven't chopped any wood." George looked around suspiciously.

"I've chopped enough. I can't work like a slave all day."

"Has anybody asked you to?" George was getting angry. "But you ought to do enough to pay your board."

"I didn't come here to chop wood anyway," Rupert replied insolently.

"I suppose you came to torment the animals," said George in a stern tone. "Why was the cat crying? Eh?"

He let Kitty slip into the hallway and gave the boy his full attention. "Answer me! The truth! Why was the dog howling? Something pretty bad had happened to him. Out with it now and don't try to lie."

Rupert was getting uncomfortable. "Those animals of yours don't know how to take a joke."

"All right," George insisted. "I want to know what your joke was."

"I didn't mean any harm. Why did the cat want to make so much fuss about it when I picked her up by the tail? And then Renni snarled at me . . . and . . ."

"And?" George was trembling with rage.

"And . . . then I gave him one."

Before the words were out of his mouth George landed a sharp slap on his jaw.

Rupert wailed, "Do you expect me to wait till he bites me?"

But his words were lost in George's raging. "You struck Renni, you wretch, the dog to whom you owe so much! The dog that nobody's ever struck in his life. You struck him, you dirty swine!"

He was slapping Rupert from one wall of the narrow woodshed to the other, regardless of his screams of pain. At last, out of breath, he pushed him away.

Mother Marie, Tanya and Bettina were standing in the entry. "Enough, my son," begged Mother Marie, whose face was pale.

But Bettina said, "That fellow couldn't possibly get the beating he deserves."

"Pack your things at once," roared George, "and get out of here as quick as you can."

Rupert ran up the stairs at top speed. He soon came

down with his bundle, whining, "You're going to pay for this."

A well-aimed kick from George's foot sent him stumbling through the front door. Renni, barking loudly, chased him to the garden gate, and then returned swinging his tail in triumph.

George told what he had caught the boy doing. And now Bettina had something to report. "He's been making fun of you from the first day on. I don't know why he confided in me. Whenever I tried to set him right about anything he always laughed. 'I know that fellow,' he'd say; 'he's no man, he's a milksop. He's a sissy that I can wind around my finger. I can make a fool of him whenever I want to.' He boasted he'd waited till the work in the garden and fields was over before he came here. 'I'll have a nice living all winter and won't have to work myself to death.' That's the kind of shirker he was behind your back."

"And you kept quiet about it all this time. Why?" For the first time George was out of patience with Bettina.

She answered in her determined way, "I don't like

to tell tales. It's a matter of principle with me. Besides, I knew you'd find out for yourself what your protégé was like. And sure enough it didn't take long."

Several weeks passed without improvement in the political situation. On the contrary the two cabinets, at home and in the neighbouring country, carried on an open war of words. The exchange of diplomatic notes became sharper and finally broke off. There was something disturbing, something fateful in this twofold silence.

"A peaceful solution seems no longer possible," Vassili intoned solemnly.

"Peaceful?" Ludmilla was not smiling now. During the last few weeks that magic smile of hers had disappeared. "Peaceful, my dear? No one thinks of peace now. On either side. Let's make arrangements to leave at once."

Vassili replied gently, "You are always right, Millie." None of the others said a word.

• • •

A few days later Tanya and Vladimir came over. Vladimir reported: "My parents, my brothers and my sister Manya are 'rats.'" His grin was ashamed and embarrassed. "They sent you their best wishes."

"Where did they go?" Mother Marie inquired.

"We don't know for sure," said Tanya. "I think they've gone to Egypt. Before they left we had a terrible row."

"They wanted us to go with them," Vladimir explained. He smiled faintly. "Now there is plenty of room in the big house . . . plenty of room."

Chapter XX

THE SNOW MELTED IN THE SPRING sunshine. The work in field and garden began again and everyone was as busy as could be.

"I wonder whether we'll ever gather the harvest," said George with a heavy heart. "Whether I'll see the flowers bloom and the cherries ripen."

In the armament factories work went on at full speed. Muster assemblies were held and the reservists were warned to be ready at a moment's notice. Classes of recruits were called before their time, and their training went on at double-quick. George got his notice to be ready for duty–the detachment to which he was detailed and to which he must report when the time came.

Early one evening after work was over he came in from the fields with Tanya and Renni. Vladimir waited until George had washed and then led him quietly into the living-room. "Tanya has gone over to our house as usual, and I want to talk with you," he whispered mysteriously.

"All right," George replied, without curiosity. "Is it something important?"

"Terribly important." Vladimir paused, and then went on very impressively, "Times are critical–and they're going to get worse, don't you think?"

"They're sure to. . . . But I don't understand. You're a foreigner and you're not liable to military service."

"No, I'm not, but . . ." There was just a glimmer of Vladimir's familiar smile. Then he grew very serious and looked George in the eye. "I beg you be honest with me, my friend, completely honest."

"I always am–with you, and, I hope, with everyone else."

Vladimir hesitated a moment longer. "Well then, do you think a lot of Bettina?"

"Silly question!" George ran his hand over Renni's head and neck. "Of course I think a lot of her."

"A very great deal?" Vladimir's voice trembled slightly.

George looked up. "What's on your mind? Go on and say it."

"Would you be angry . . . if another . . . if I . . . ?"

"Say, do you think this is a surprise to me?" George laughed.

"We just wanted to know whether we had your permission."

"Who's 'we'?"

"Why, Bettina and I."

"You need fear no objection from me. But how about your father and mother?"

Vladimir frowned. "I told them about it as they were leaving. They are neither for nor against it. Their last word was that I should do as I pleased."

"Well then, I wish you happiness."

Rather unexpectedly Vladimir was not at all sentimental over it. He called the dog to him and as Renni put out his paw to shake hands he murmured, "You are happy, Renni. Only you. . . . And God knows how long it will last."

There was no change in the relationship of the five people. They lived and they worked together as before. Vladimir and Bettina spoke occasionally of preparations for their marriage.

"We shall need very little," said Vladimir. "There are plenty of things over at our house."

And Bettina said, "We won't need anything at all." The others offered no suggestion.

Spring moved on, drawing into summer.

One day Nickel came over with Hector. He had news. "Our dogs will soon have work to do."

"Is that why you're in such good humour?" said Mother Marie, petting Hector.

"Well, good humour helps more than bad." Nickel

laughed. He delivered a little lecture. "Fate has set itself in motion, hasn't it? Is there anything I can do to protect myself against it? I, or George, or any of us? Just look here, now: Not even these governments snarling in each other's faces can stop it. Am I right? These statesmen that act so high and mighty and imagine they're guiding events–they haven't the slightest suspicion that they're themselves under a higher law. Fate, my dear lady, fate. There's no way to resist it. Am I right?"

"If . . ." George began.

"You're about to say something silly." Nickel cut him short. "There's no such thing as *if* when you're talking of fate. Not while a thing's happening, and certainly not after it's happened. Could anybody have stopped the World War? Not by a long shot. It would have broken out even without the assassinations at Sarajevo. Just think it over: That young Serbian–his name was Princip, wasn't it?–with two bullets he killed two people, the heir apparent and his wife. That double killing with one revolver you'll hardly find repeated in the history of firearms. The young man must have been too excited to take good aim, and he didn't have time. Yet each bullet took effect. Fate! Clear case of fate. Am I right?"

"How many human lives were destroyed in the World War?" asked Mother Marie.

Nickel's laugh was short and harsh. "Exactly as many as fate marked for death. Not one more. Not one less. And those who must die this summer–who on earth can say *why* they must be sacrificed? No more do we know of that than we can tell which are doomed to fall. Fate decides. Dark, mysterious, unfathomable, but all-powerful fate."

"I shudder at the thought," said Mother Marie.

"I've got over shuddering," Nickel cried. "It does no good. I can only laugh over a world gone mad. It helps me keep my balance. Yes, the world has undoubtedly gone mad, dear lady, but there's a mysterious law at work. This world of ours is coming to an end. It's certainly going to smash. Anybody can see that, can't he? And the new world which will come into being is a world we'll never live to see, a world we can't even imagine."

"The old world of castles and palaces," interrupted George, "the world in which a handful rolled in luxury and the masses starved . . . that world seems gone forever."

"Do you regret it?" Nickel asked.

"I–regret?" George was almost angry. "When millions go hungry there's no justice in pomp and luxury for the few."

"But we can't be too sure about the future, my friend. This very day the upstarts who have grown great indulge themselves and revel as the kings and princes used to do. Who knows whether the future will really change things."

"You're not consistent. And aren't you exaggerating now?"

"Maybe. I don't know. One minute I'm full of hope. The next I'm all gloom."

Hector and Kitty were rolling and wrestling on the floor. Renni stood near them, ears high, nose down, turning his head alternately from one to the other, ready at any moment to take a part in the game. But he found no chance. Hector had Kitty's head in his mouth again and she lay on her back kicking with hind feet at her captor till at last he set her free. Before either of the dogs could seize her she slipped away and landed on the window sill with one jump; as the dogs reared up toward her, barking, she gave a flying leap to the top of the high clothespress, quite beyond their reach.

There she sat with a lofty, indifferent look on her face and began busily making her toilet. Renni and Hector played for a few minutes and then stretched out, each at his master's feet.

"These fellows–" said George, slapping Renni on the flank–"they live in a world that's always happy."

"A world where they have no will of their own."

"That's the reason for it," George agreed. "Without will of their own. They're absolutely loyal. They never change. You can't shake them."

"Well, we're true to our duty, too, and we have no will of our own," said Nickel. "You and I, we ought to be happy. We and our dogs go to war, not to kill men, but to help them, to save them from death."

"Thank God," sighed Mother Marie.

When Nickel had left, George set about putting his equipment in order. "War may begin any day now," he said.

Tanya went to see Vogg. "I'd like to buy a dog. If possible, one about a year old."

The breeder looked at her sharply. "Don't you belong to that Russian family?" She admitted it, only to be told, "I've no dog for you."

"But it isn't for me."

Vogg was suspicious and stuck to his guns. "I haven't any dogs."

But Tanya insisted, "You're going to sell me a dog."

Vogg asked ironically, "Does the old man think he can worry along with one watch dog now?"

Tanya laughed. "I wasn't thinking of my father. He has gone off on a long journey and I don't know when he'll be back."

She went on to explain that she would very likely live with George's mother in case he and Renni went to war. "Mother Marie must not be left without a dog. It would be too lonesome for her."

"How do you stand on the subject of whipping?"

"Exactly the way George does."

Vogg became confidential. "You seem a nice girl. Come, I'll let you see Laddie. Perhaps you'll suit him."

He took her to the kennels. The old breeder's idea that the prospective owner must stand the test of a dog's approval amused Tanya. She thought it charming. They went into the room with doors opening on the garden. It re-echoed with joyful yelping and barking. A mother dog sprang up from her nest where she was suckling three puppies, drew hesitantly near Tanya, growled a little, and smelled her over carefully. Tanya stood perfectly still. The dog began waving her tail. Tanya patted her gently and begged, "Show me your babies." Then the dog went calmly back to her bed and stretched out.

But Tanya did not get to look around, for in a second she was surrounded by a whole pack. She did not even notice that Vogg had left her alone. Eight or nine police dogs, brown, black, yellow, of all ages and sizes, crowded around her, leaped up to put their forepaws on her shoulders, tried to lick her hands and face and treated her as if she were a long-expected guest. Tanya did not defend herself. In a few minutes she was scarcely to be seen in the tumbling mass of dogs.

Two or three were evidently the youngest, as she could tell by their prankish ways. One of them stood out because he was a little larger than the others. He had a beautiful tawny coat like a lion's. Tanya liked him particularly and the dog seemed to like her in return.

Then Vogg came in, helped her out of the tangle, got the dogs quiet and said, "Well, it's just as I thought. Laddie likes you."

The lion-coloured dog crouched low, sprang high into the air, and then started dashing around in a mad circle.

"Is that Laddie?" asked Tanya, staggering from a new outburst of the dog's affection.

"Laddie!" cried the breeder, "that will do. Come here!" Laddie danced around with twinkling legs and ran up with his tail swinging violently.

"You see, he has a way with him." Vogg put his hand under the dog's head and said to him, "This is your mistress. Pay attention." There was a happy gleam in Laddie's dark eyes.

The pedigree which Tanya received showed that he lacked two months of being a year old.

When she reached the house, the delight of expectation changed to alarm. She found only Mother Marie there.

"George had to report at a moment's notice!" the mother sobbed. "Bettina and Vladimir are taking him to the station. I couldn't bear to go."

Tanya turned pale. "Did he . . . didn't he . . . leave any word for me?"

"All he said was that you knew how he felt."

Tanya burst into sobs. Laddie sat disconsolate, not knowing what to do. He whimpered softly.

After Tanya had with an effort controlled her feelings, she said, "This is one of Vogg's dogs. I bought him, so the house wouldn't seem so empty while Renni's away . . ." She paused, choked, and then went on more quietly, "I wasn't prepared to find everyone gone."

Mother Marie petted Laddie. "I'm so glad you're here, old fellow. So very glad. I'm not being disloyal to Renni! I couldn't be! But you'll be a comfort and a sort of keepsake of Renni . . . of my son," she added, striving to be calm.

Kitty came in to see what it was all about. She stood facing Laddie, her tail twitching, to let him sniff her over. He did the job thoroughly. Then he looked at Tanya with a question in his eye. She stroked Kitty and preached him a sermon. "See this nice kitten, this darling kitten? You must be good to her! You must make friends with her! Will you?"

Laddie listened closely, his head straight up and down, his big ears pricked up, his plume waving. Then, ducking down with his fore knees, he gave a short bark, challenging Kitty to play. She struck out at him with her soft paws and, as they started tearing around the room, she took the chance and sprang on his neck. He dropped to the floor. They rolled about together in a funny sham battle. They had made friends.

Chapter XXI

MEANWHILE GEORGE AND Renni had arrived at the railway station. Bettina and Vladimir followed them through the huge crowd which filled the great building to bursting.

Crying of women, screaming of children, shouts of the soldiers, singing, echoes rolling madly down from the roof of iron and glass, whistling of locomotives, clanging of iron wheels, clashing of cars one against the other—the confusion bewildered, the gigantic noise deafened. A thick haze lay over the excited, frightened crowd. The evil smell of gasoline, of coal smoke, of clothing, of food, of beer, of bad tobacco, had a sort of stupefying effect. Every individual here was, in a way of speaking, extinguished. The soul was cramped and crushed. It seemed to shrivel, to creep into itself, no longer capable of effort.

After the first few minutes George felt the brunt of this. Vladimir's cheerful words fell on his ears without effect, slipped off his mind as if they had no meaning. Only Bettina's glance caused a little twitching at his heart. Mechanically he kept hold on Renni, who crowded anxiously against him. He fought his way through the mass of humanity, swaying in waves of a feverish storm. Their resignation was broken by wails from the women, by loud cries from the men. They may have tried to seem assured, but they were really pursued by a secret fear.

At the car he returned Vladimir's handclasp only half-consciously. He held Bettina's hand a moment, and heard her say, "Good-bye. Hurry home."

He did not know whether or not he answered her, but he helped Renni climb the steps.

The train set itself slowly in motion, with a barely audible sound, for the singing and yelling of the soldiers and all the bedlam outside swelled into thunderous volume, and only the shrill whistle of the engine could be heard above it. The living wall of people, wildly waving farewell, was gradually left behind. Their voices died away, and the soldiers stopped calling to them out of the windows. The train rolled into the open country.

The land lay fair in the soft sunshine, the peaceful peasant homes seemed to smile gently, the cattle grazed on the meadows, leafy trees lifted their tender green, doves fluttered in swarms, and from the church towers came the drone of bells broken by distance and the rumble of the train.

For a while everyone kept silence, as though they all, stowed away in this car like baggage, realised of a sudden that now the partings had really been said, a farewell to their old peaceful existence, perhaps forever. And when the soldiers began to sing and to chatter, some still were silent, pensive, sunk in memories and dreams.

Renni wore his Red Cross band on his back, George his on one arm. The men made way for them. The decision which meant war or peace had not come yet. But when George reached his destination, the rumour went round that the ultimatum from the opposing nation would expire tomorrow. The word "enemy" was heard now.

Next morning came the order to march. So it was war!

"It was bound to be," they said. "It couldn't be avoided."

In vain George racked his brain. Why should war be unavoidable? Why was it natural? He could think of no plausible reason. "I guess I don't know enough about it. I've never thought these things out." He stroked Renni. "Our job, old boy, is just to help the unfortunate. That's what we'll do, eh?"

Renni made his full agreement known by the look in his eye and the wag of his tail.

At Sanitary headquarters everything went as if by

clockwork, like everything else in the army. George reported briefly, in a very businesslike manner. The orders he got were equally curt. A surgeon, a man no longer young, when he heard George's name and Renni's raised his head and said briefly, "I've heard of you." That was all.

A number of dogs, perhaps a score, were on hand, all with Red Cross bands. They waved their tails in welcome to one another, but stood quietly, without straining at the leashes, each beside his handler. Renni seemed visibly changed, more serious, less playful, perhaps not so affectionate as before, but dependable, and full of a tense expectancy.

Nickel stepped up, tapped George on the shoulder. "The fun's over now." Renni and Hector exchanged greetings. "We and our dogs . . ." Nickel blinked and tried to smile, but the effort ended in dismal failure.

"There'll be blood flowing, perhaps, before the day's over . . . a lot of it. Well, as I always say, fate is fate."

George only nodded.

• • •

Finally came the word. Already the enemy had launched an invasion farther east, and orders were to march. The army moved over the border. Into the enemy country!

These villages, these fields, these meadows! . . . So that was what the enemy country was like. It looked much like home. The peasant houses, the barns, the stables—all empty. Before the invasion they had evacuated them all. They had thrown up hasty embankments and dug ditches as tank traps. Scouts and engineers, sent out ahead, found the ditches and hurriedly tried to fill them. The barbed-wire entanglements were flattened out by the armoured cars and trucks.

Then the artillery shells began to explode, sinking deep into the earth, hurling dirt high into the air, and human limbs and bodies with it. And as the dust and smoke thinned out, you could see them start slowly to fall back again to earth. Bodies lay around twisted into grotesque shapes. Even the hardiest shuddered at the sight.

The first sacrifices to War.

Then came the hollow droning of propellers. Enemy

planes soared high overhead. They dropped low, dark missiles, which struck the earth and exploded with an ear-splitting detonation. A wicked sound. Earth and fragments of steel scattered everywhere. Anti-aircraft guns replied. Everyone looked for a shelter. George and Renni found one. "Thank God!" He thought he was saying it to himself, but he had said it aloud. The bellowing of the guns had drowned his voice. He reached out his hand for Renni, who pressed close against him, and patted him reassuringly, for the dog, realising that this was in deadly earnest, was trembling from head to foot.

"There now, Renni," George said, trying to cheer him. "Good old Renni, don't be afraid!" Hardly had he spoken when he noticed that his own knees were shaking, that his throat was dry.

A squadron flew out to meet the enemy and drive them off. A dogfight. Bark of machine guns, flashes from gun muzzles, whistle of falling bombs. Then an enemy plane staggered, slipped sidewise, crashed. A second turned nose down and dived sickeningly. Now one of their own fell. George in an excitement he could hardly control, was still fascinated by the magnificent show, a sort of drama of heroic grandeur. It was not for some time that he realised this spectacle was the ravaging of death. When the two squadrons drew apart, it struck him with full force, this dreadful thing that had happened here.

A silence followed, shattered now and then by the rattling of tanks, by artillery fire, by the clash of weapons and the tread of tens of thousands. A moment of comparative quiet after the infernal tumult. A voice saying, "That was only the beginning, only a small beginning."

George turned around and saw a mass of pallid faces, some smiling convulsively, most of them staring straight ahead. He did not know who had spoken, but an echo in his heart kept repeating, "This is only the beginning, only a small beginning."

March, march, march.

Evening began to fall, turned to darkness, a gloom which settled on everything, as though it wanted to cast a veil over the horrors of strife, over the bloody strife between men who did not know one another, who had never done anything to injure one another till this day. The stars twinkled peacefully in the heavens. The scent of freshly upturned earth hovered over their heads, mingled with the traces of burnt powder which drifted past from the exploded bombs and the fire from the anti-aircraft guns.

But the sheltering gloom was of no avail. Rockets lighted up the sky, and searchlights stabbed the dark.

Away at the very front infantry fire began to clatter. A quiver of expectancy ran along the ranks. No one asked a question, no one risked a guess.

The firing ceased.

March, march, march. Till late into the night. At last a few hasty bites of food, then the heavy sleep of exhaustion under the open sky. Renni, lying against George's breast, sighed deeply, twice. He fell to dreaming, with the slack twitching of the legs, the high-pitched, choking whine that dreaming dogs are used to make. George did not awaken.

Chapter XXII

DAY AFTER DAY THE BATTLE raged. When there were pauses in the fighting, cries could be heard as the wounded were examined, lifted and carried to the dressing-stations. The staff of the Sanitary Corps showed a remarkable skill, often hidden under a rough manner. There were many too worn out to try to conceal their weariness; and others who wore their weariness openly, not caring how it showed.

For the present there was no attempt to bury the

dead. There would be time for that later on . . . and if not . . . Whenever it was mentioned there was a great shrugging of shoulders.

They had a name for the work of the dogs who went about searching for signs of life in the motionless forms; they called it "gleaning."

Renni was frightened at the dead bodies. At first he started back from them in terror. He did not seem to understand what he saw, yet in his inmost being he knew what death was. He trembled with fear, and crept forward in a sort of anguish. When he found a man seriously wounded, doubts plagued him whether the man still lived and he would turn to his master for help. George had no strength to share with him, for he was himself too shaken by pity and horror and a sort of tremendous astonishment. He had to make a painful effort to collect his wits, to gain at least a halfway control of himself.

Once when they came back in the night from their scouting, they were both so unnerved they could not think of sleep.

The battle had raged all day, and had taken more than its fair share of life. George and his comrades had divided up the field, and each gone his way with his dog without concern for the others.

Their army had won the field, had moved forward and was now far ahead. Artillery rumbled in the distance. Rockets glared. The percussions of aerial bombs, shooting up from the earth, looked like sheet lightning. One had the impression of a terrific storm, whose lash was nerve-shattering.

The surgeons worked away at the several first-aid stations, worked in great haste, in swift silence, full of pity and yet irritated by a sense of helplessness before all the suffering.

Going off a little to one side, George sat down with Renni. Appalling sounds came to them from the first-aid station. They sat in the dark, on the bare earth, and looked off toward the storm of battle, raging away in the distance.

George gave a deep, hopeless sigh. Renni looked around at him.

"Yes, old man, we're helping," said George softly. "We two are helping as much as we can. But help, real help, for such things as this, that lies beyond our power."

Renni wagged his tail, so that the noise of it on the ground sounded like ghostly whispering.

"What we're doing," George continued, "is so little, so pitifully little . . . no matter how we try . . . no matter if we give our all. It comes to nothing. The suffering of men is so great, so immeasurably great."

Then Renni laid his head in George's lap, as if to comfort him. The gentle tapping of his tail took on a sound like something out of the good earth, like something well known, intimate, like a kind of soothing speech.

George's hand stroked Renni's head while his words went on: "And still . . . and still we're necessary, you and I." He talked to him as though to a fellow man. He opened his heart to him, poured out the burden of his sorrow, sure of being understood; or perhaps it made little difference whether he was understood or not. George had to say what was in his heart, and so he went on with his soliloquy. He kept stroking Renni's silky forehead, and talking softly. "Yes, we two are needed . . . and we are useful . . . in spite of everything, my dog. . . . We bring a man now and then out of this inferno . . . help him in his helplessness . . . not many, a few. In war people cease to be persons, separate individuals. So long as men are under fire, can keep on their feet, can go on shooting and charging like robots, they're not themselves at all; they forget they have a life of their own, they forget their work, their hopes, their sorrows, their joys. They simply have to forget it all. They must. They're only senseless atoms. Atoms in a strange and terrible compound. But a mighty will runs through them, a sort of mass intoxication, a compelling force to overcome the power of the enemy, to reach an objective, and this force melts them all together into one living whole . . . victory, fame! Yes, yes, my good Renni, you know nothing of the might, the soaring aspiration of this mob spirit."

He was silent a while. He pressed the warm body of the dog closer to him, felt the tenderness, the perfect love, which flowed into him from it. He responded to it. "We two at least can see the other side. We care for the poor fellows who lie wounded on the ground. We carry them out, and they . . . well, when they wake up, when they're put to bed, they cease to be atoms, then. They're men again, persons, individuals . . . with a fate of their own . . . all too often a fate distorted out of all semblance of itself."

He sighed. "Oh, God! War leaves all its victims wrecked in body, soul or spirit, or all three." He breathed deeply. "Only a very few, only the most robust come out of this mad horror unscathed. Or do any so? Who knows?"

George stopped talking. His head sank wearily on his breast, but he did not sleep. Renni, his muzzle in George's lap, slumbered soundly in spite of his uncomfortable position.

The distant thunder was now stilled. The surgeons at the dressing-station had finished their work. The ambulances clattered off to the hospitals with their broken burdens.

Silence brooded over the dark plain. The stars

shimmered in the heavens. It was not long till morning. Then, high in the air, sounded the song of birds, a trilling magically lovely, a glad, melodious outburst.

George lifted his eyes astonished. Renni awoke on the instant, shook himself, looked up eagerly at the sky. Both listened to the birds' song, ringing down from up there in a miracle of music. In the first grey of dawn they could not distinguish the larks soaring among the clouds. George could only make out that the ground before them, trampled, pitted with craters, strewn with the dead, had once been tilled land, a cultivated field.

The tiny larks, in some miraculous fashion left unharmed in all this horror, had risen above it and greeted the rising sun as on any happy morning.

Renni wagged his tail gently, and stared upward. George had to wipe his eyes, for they were wet with tears.

Chapter XXIII

AT LAST THERE CAME A DAY WHEN the murderous roar of battle died down and that night it ceased entirely.

The quiet was uncanny, disturbing. Still a deep sigh of relief passed through the ranks. All around, near and far, great fires were burning, dyeing the black sky with red reflections. The steady march forward paused for a while.

On the verge of exhaustion, George and his comrades of the Sanitary Corps, with the rear guard of the army, made their way to a small town which had been partly destroyed. Many of the houses were heaps of ruins; others had one side torn off, or whole stories cut in half, with what had once been rooms jutting out into the open air.

But it was the next day before they noted this destruction. That night when they marched in, it was quite dark, for the light plant was in ruins. Nobody knew or cared what shape the little town was in. Here was the luxury of which they had been long deprived. Within them was only one desire, driving out every other thought. Sleep! Sleep!

When George and Renni awoke they found themselves in what must have been a showroom. Empty counters, a long desk, but no chairs, benches or tables.

Other trainers and their dogs were still asleep. When they began to awaken they looked around in a sort of daze, stretched out comfortably again on the smooth floor boards and took a long time about getting up.

"At least it's dry here," someone called. No one answered, no one laughed. They had lost the knack of laughter. Two or three, George among them, got up to look through the building and see if there were anyone around. It was all as empty as the showroom in which they had spent the night. Whoever had lived here had fled.

In one story after another the apartments seemed practically unharmed. On the second floor a wire-haired fox terrier flew at George, snapping his teeth, and then immediately ran behind the bed, where he lay whimpering in fear. George tried to coax him out with friendly words, but the terrier snarled angrily. Then Renni lay down flat on the floor, stuck his muzzle under the bed–there wasn't room for more of him in the narrow space. He must have whispered something soothing to the shy, frightened animal. The terrier crept out, a changed dog. He played gaily with Renni and made no resistance when George took him in his arms.

"You poor, lost puppy!" said George. "You've a right to be surly when strangers come bursting in this way. But we're not strangers any longer, are we? You're not lost now and we'll all be good friends together–you, Renni and I."

The terrier listened with a look of deep wisdom on his face and his stubby ears pricked up. He had been sick with lonesomeness, but now seemed suddenly free, perfectly happy at having company again. In a few minutes he was eating and drinking greedily; he must have been tortured by hunger and thirst for days.

They went on exploring the house. George found a bathroom and seized the welcome chance of a bath for himself and Renni. They needed it after these weeks of dirt. There were plenty of soap and towels.

When they went down again to the display-room the dogs were holding a get-acquainted party.

"Do you understand what's going on?" Renni asked Hector. He thought of him as an old friend and had great respect for his wisdom because he was so much older.

"Nobody can understand it," Hector answered. "I've never seen anything like it."

Another dog said, "We're a long way from home. Far from everything we've been used to. How can we take it?"

Still another chimed in. "It isn't the way it used

to be. These things used to last only three days. Now there's no end to the business."

Renni added, "In the old days some would be bleeding but only a few. Now everyone we find is that way."

Hector said, sad and worried, "And most of them are dead, and we can't help them at all. I never saw any dead before this. It's a terrible thing to see the dead."

"You get used to it," put in an old dog with unusually long ears.

"No," contradicted Renni, "I can never get used to it."

"Nor I."

"I know I can't," Hector asserted.

"I only said that to make you feel better," Long-Ears assured them. "The sight and scent of the dead really fill me with fear and horror."

"Why in the world do they do such things?" sighed Renni.

"I believe they've all gone crazy," was Hector's opinion.

"Impossible," said Long-Ears. "How could they all go crazy at once?"

"Perhaps it's contagious."

"Nothing of the sort. They're simply fighting one another."

"Fighting for what? Don't they have food, homes–everything they want? . . . Why should they fight?"

Long-Ears wrinkled his nose scornfully. "What about us? Each of us has food, a home, pretty much everything he wants, and yet we've all been in plenty of fights, haven't we?"

"Yes," Renni admitted, "but that's different."

"Well, we're only dogs."

Renni said, "We dogs fight only when we're insulted, or when we're challenged, or when we're attacked."

"There must have been a strange lot of terrible insults and challenges going around to call for huge fights like these," said Hector. "They have been getting ready for them a long time. Otherwise we wouldn't have learned our business and practised at it. Such things must be secrets of a high order. Anyhow, they're beyond me."

Fox sat on his haunches in their midst, listening tensely, the richer for their remarkable experiences.

• • •

Meanwhile the dog-trainers were talking things over. Young Wier pounded with his fist on the desk which served for a table, so that the metal plates and tin cups danced and clattered. "We're winning! We're winning! That's all that matters." He pulled his dog over to him and roared in his ear, "Do you hear? Rascal, do you hear? Victory is ours!"

Rascal stood limp under the hands of his master, who now began to sing a soldier song. He sang alone, with only the accompaniment of Rascal's yelps and Fox's barking. Wier let go his dog, stopped singing and looked around. "Why don't you join in?"

Marly shrugged his shoulders.

Greenow, a thoughtful man, said, "Maybe we're thinking of the lives it costs."

"But so long as we're winning, it's worth all it costs, isn't it?" Wier demanded.

Greenow answered earnestly, "Yes . . . if we always win . . . perhaps."

"Well," Nickel remarked, "I guess a man might think

that, so long as he isn't a part of the cost himself." He glanced around. "Who knows whether we're going to stay here long enough to get a good rest?" No one knew.

"If we keep on advancing and advancing," Karger reasoned, "I figure we're winning. But we don't know a thing about it. We can't find out anything. We just grope around in the dark. We really ought . . ."

"The Chief of Staff really ought to keep Corporal Karger better informed," cried Marly.

The others laughed, and they laughed again when Karger said, "It would be a pretty smart thing for him to do."

"And you–" Nickel nudged George–"haven't you anything to say?"

George drew a deep breath. "I wish we were all back home."

A troop of prisoners marched past the windows. The men inside scarcely noticed them. They went back to sleep. Only George went out on the street. The prisoners were marching steadily along. Under their tan they were pale and thin. Some seemed completely sunk.

They looked sad, or desperate, or almost insane. Others made no attempt to conceal their relief. You could read on their faces how happy they were to have escaped the dangers of war.

One of them, a man about forty, stepped over and patted Renni. "I've a dog like that at home," he said to George. Renni wagged his tail in a particularly friendly way.

George asked, "Do you think often of your home?"

The man looked at him in astonishment "Well . . . no . . . can't say I do . . . but . . ."

He ran back to his place in the ranks, turned around several times and waved his hand. The soldier on guard had ordered him, "Don't stop there. March on!" But it had not sounded harsh. Rather like a gentle warning. George smiled at the soldier, who saluted him.

"This prisoner," he thought, "probably has a wife and children. But still he doesn't think of home. War cut him off from all he knew and cherished. He was face to face with death, ready to suffer it . . . and only Renni reminded him that he had once lived a life of his own.

"And I?" George felt a sudden shock of surprise, for he had forgotten home too. The wish he had expressed to Nickel had come without thought or will or feeling. He had not been thinking of his mother or of Tanya, of his garden or his fields. He felt ashamed. Was this man a warning to him? But why should he need warning? He stooped down and slapped Renni on the back. The dog looked up at him, frankly, cheerfully, gratefully.

"We've been used to something better than this, old boy, haven't we? Now we've got to put up with it as best we can. Thinking and remembering won't do us any good."

Renni swung his tail in vigorous agreement.

George looked into the dog's clear eyes. "All we must think of is this: with every wounded man that we rescue we do some good. Whether he's a friend or a foe, it's all the same to you, partner, isn't it? And to me. We have no enemies."

He let the dog slip to the ground. Renni gave a leap or two to show his love and joy, but quickly controlled himself and took his regulation position by his master's side.

George went on to himself: "Memory leads to longing and makes a man unfit for service. This war business swallows up memory completely. Thank God for it."

But the cataract of events which roared around him soon diverted his thoughts. He had walked to the central square of the town. The poor inhabitants had been in hiding. Some of them had been chased from their hiding-places and others had come creeping out of their own free will. They stood now huddled close to one another in their anguish–old men, women, girls, weeping children–and they trembled at the unknown fate which their fears painted for them.

Standing on a box, a captain addressed them in a loud voice. "People! Have no fear! No harm will be done you. Your property will not be disturbed. Is your mayor here?"

Silence. Then a woman's wild, broken cry: "He ran away."

The captain nodded. "Thank you." He went on, sternly now, "You must give up your weapons, firearms, swords, knives. Any attempt to hide them will be punishable by death. Also, any hostile demonstration against the troops and any disobedience of military orders. Is that understood?"

Another short silence. Then again the woman's wild, broken voice, pitched a little higher this time: "Yes, sir! Oh, yes!"

A few men also called out, "Yes! We understand!"

Again the captain nodded. "Dismissed. All of you who behave yourselves are in perfect safety. You can depend on that. Open your shops. We'll pay cash for everything we buy from you. But business houses that are deserted will be confiscated, and all that is in them."

He made a gesture of dismissal with his right arm. "All right now. Go to your homes and be perfectly calm."

Once more the woman's voice was heard: "Our homes! Half of them are in ruins. Our homes!" There were bitterness and suppressed sobbing in her tones.

Shrugging his shoulders, the captain stepped down.

Meanwhile Nickel had joined George, and Fox had left his side to go sniffing among the people. Fox did it carefully and thoroughly. When he came back, he sat down beside Renni and looked on attentively as the crowd dispersed. He had made up his mind.

George picked up the wriggling little tike and held him in his arms. You're right, Foxy. Stick to Renni and me."

Suddenly, in some distant street three shots barked out, close together.

"Shotguns," Nickel decided.

They listened. Another shot.

Nickel said, "One of our army pistols."

A crowd was approaching. Soldiers shouted angrily. Women screamed and wailed. The crowd came on.

"They'll be shot without ceremony," came the words, and then: "It would be a fine idea–to let them murder us–wouldn't it?"

Someone called out, "They're crazy, simply crazy. It's the craziest thing ever."

"Fanatics," said Nickel to George. "The thing's perfectly clear. They shot at our men from some house."

George saw two soldiers led by, supported by comrades. One was bleeding from the arm, the other from the shoulder. They staggered a little as they walked. Their faces were pale, and fear and astonishment were written on them. They were being taken to the dressing-station. Behind them came the snipers, in chains. Three men, one a hunchback, the second a greybeard with wildly rumpled hair, the third perfectly bald. Then a young girl and a pretty little boy. Their faces were the colour of ashes, their eyes dead, their expressions dazed. Only the boy looked ahead with eager eyes as though he were going through a fascinating adventure. The escort of soldiers, guns at the ready and bayonets fixed, surrounded them like a moving hedge, shutting them off from the swarming mob. Despite the confusion and excitement, the crowd kept solemn silence. Now and then a low moan, a wailing sob, nothing more.

"Are you going to shoot the child, too?" A man's voice screamed the question. The wailing rose. No answer.

Two officers came up and stopped near George, a colonel and a lieutenant.

"It's a terrible shame such an idiotic thing had to

happen," the colonel growled. "Take them out beyond the lines. Over there at the edge of town. The third battalion is on guard there. Take them a few hundred steps beyond the pickets and get it over." His voice sounded tense, hoarse. "Oh, yes. Set the boy free first. Don't let him see what happens." He paused. "Somebody'll look after him all right."

In a queer, unnatural voice, the lieutenant asked, "And the girl?"

"Clear case with her."

"But it's perfectly plain she's innocent," stammered the lieutenant.

"But she's of age." The colonel choked out the words. "Adult. I can't spare her. I dare not. It's really neglect of duty to let the boy. . . ." He spoke from between clenched teeth. "You know the law. Two of our men have been wounded . . . short shrift . . . nothing to be done about it. Go, Lieutenant. It's hard on you, and hard on me too. Go and may God help you!"

"At your orders, Colonel." The lieutenant staggered a little as he saluted and withdrew.

At the same moment the colonel started off in the other direction, but Renni stopped him, dashing around him, waving his tail, trying to leap up on him.

"What! What!" sputtered the colonel. Then he recognised the dog. "Why, Renni, is it you? My old friend and rescuer, God bless you!" Renni, his body arched in joy, felt his back slapped and licked the hand that caressed him.

The colonel looked about. "Corporal, you remember me? I had an accident last year during manœuvres." He pointed to his ankle. "I was a major then." He smiled wanly. "It's good to see you again."

George, shocked and shaken, could not say a word.

"Renni remembers me," said the colonel. "Yes, Renni, you're a fine old dog." And he stroked the beautiful head. "You, Corporal, I suppose you've forgotten me."

"Certainly not, Colonel," George got out with an effort. . . . His eyes followed the firing squad as it marched off in the distance. "Renni's lucky. He doesn't take this in."

The echo of a volley rolled past.

Chapter XXIV

THE FORTUNES OF WAR CHANGED, for a while at least. They had to evacuate the little town. Swift retreat. So far as there can be order in such a situation—and the staff maintained that the withdrawal went according to plan and in the best of order—the operation was made without overmuch confusion. Still, enemy planes spattered the close-packed masses with bombs. They would be driven off by anti-aircraft, but ten or twenty bombs exploding in the dense ranks were enough to cover the field with dead and wounded. Screams and shrill cries, moans and groans mingled with the roar of the crashing bombs. When a plane was hit and plunged to earth, it would bury the soldiers who were not quick enough to get out from under its blazing ruins.

In his eagerness, Renni ran into one such spot. The moaning of the men on the ground called him. He ignored the missiles raining from the air, the shell fragments falling back from the fire of the anti-aircraft batteries. Fox darted after him. George ran out to bring them both back from the danger spot. For the first time Renni refused to obey until the command had been repeated. Even then he did it grudgingly. And for the first time George had to speak sternly, even harshly, to his dog. He was himself in danger but thought little of that. His fear was all for the dog. He ran as fast as he could with Renni on the leash. Fox galloped cheerfully along beside them.

Once in the shelter at the dressing-station, George heaped Renni with reproaches. Humbly, unused to the rough tone, Renni crept on his belly to his master's feet. Fox sat upright, put his forepaws together and moved them up and down as if he were praying forgiveness for his friend.

George couldn't help smiling. "All right, little Foxy. I'm not angry any longer."

Fox hopped confidently to George's lap where he curled up comfortably while George spoke more gently to Renni. "What made you do that? You got in too big a hurry, old man. Much too big a hurry. What would have happened if a bullet had hit you? You'd have dropped dead as a stone. And then you never could have helped again."

Renni straightened up, sat down on his haunches, wagged his tail eagerly, looked George straight in the eyes, and listened attentively. "You're brave, old boy, very, very brave. But you must wait till I send you out. Then you can hunt. Hunt as much as you please. I'll have to lead you on a leash if you're going to forget, and I can't let you run free any longer. I have so much confidence in you, Renni, and you know how I love you."

"Why, that dog understands every word," said Nickel.

Renni let out a whine of joy and threw himself on George who could not dodge the attack and fell over backward.

At once Renni and Fox were all over him, washing his hands and face.

The heavy artillery and the armoured cars got mixed up with the infantry and the supply trains, and wild confusion was about to result. Higher officers took a hand to avoid panic. Lines were reformed, and the episode, which might have spelled disaster, passed over harmlessly.

Nickel said to George, "You see . . . discipline's needed more when you're losing than when you're winning."

"Oh," cried Marly, "we're not beaten yet!"

Nickel laughed grimly. "But we can't say we're on top now."

"See here," Wier protested. "I differ with you. We licked them once and we'll lick them again. We've been thrown back a little, but that doesn't mean a thing."

George said quietly, "Lucky the enemy planes didn't attack during the mix-up."

"Right!" Marly agreed. "You can tell from that that the enemy's not in good shape."

When they halted early in the evening for a new disposition of their forces, the Sanitary Corps had reached the ruins of a village which had been repeatedly stormed, lost and recaptured. They were to be stationed here. The handlers and their tired dogs enjoyed the peace of this hour under the open sky. The trainers sat apart from one another, without speaking. This interlude of idleness did them good. Tense expectancy, the excitement which had endured up to now, gave way to sleepy relaxation of nerve and muscle.

Then a pigeon fluttered past. She flew along very close to the dogs, alighted right in front of Renni, and walked back and forth nodding her little head and glancing warily to this side and that. Fox, who had been lying full-length beside Renni, charged at her. She flew up in alarm, but not very high, and came back to earth right beside Renni. Again and again Fox made her fly but every time she returned to Renni in this way. George finally put the terrier on the leash and now Fox had to look on helplessly as the pigeon strutted back and forth. He quivered, yelped impatiently, and at length lapsed into an astonished silence. But his quivering went on.

George and the other trainers were amazed at the pigeon. She tripped closer and closer to Renni until she almost touched him, looking up at him with sidewise motions of her head.

Renni bent down, sniffed at her curiously and thoroughly, and she took it in utmost serenity. She seemed to have no fear, but rather to enjoy Renni's puffing breath. She rocked her back, gleaming sapphire and gold, from side to side, as though it were being stroked, and closed her eyes for a few seconds. Renni had no idea of doing her harm. His investigation satisfied him. A complete and friendly understanding prevailed between dog and dove.

"It's as if she wanted to bring him a message," laughed Nickel.

"Perhaps she has," George answered.

Now with two strokes of her light grey pinions the pigeon swung herself up on Renni's head. He calmly allowed her to perch there as though they had agreed on it.

"I bet it's a carrier pigeon," said Marly.

"See if you can catch her," Nickel advised.

The dove crouched without struggling, as George took gentle hold of her. To his astonishment Renni growled softly at him.

"But, Renni, don't you know who I am?" George reproached him. He examined the pigeon which lay perfectly quiet on his hands.

"No band on her foot," he reported. "No roll of paper under her feathers. Just an ordinary country pigeon."

Waving her wings, she balanced on his finger, which her claws clasped tightly. Renni looked at them, not growling now, but still not quite at ease. George lowered his hand with care. The dove fluttered down on Renni's head again and he stretched out satisfied.

"Well now, what does this mean?" Nickel asked. "Where did she come from?"

"Why, of course I don't know where she came from," said George. "War frightens and confuses a lot of animals, numbs them. Dogs and cats wander around in bewilderment, looking for refuge. It's as clear as can be that's what this lone dove was seeking."

"And finds it with your dog." Nickel smiled. "Maybe you're right. One thing's certain: man and beast trust Renni."

Renni turned over on his side. The dove was now perched so close to his ear that he kept twitching it. She seemed to realise she was bothering him there, so she moved on to his neck. With great ceremony she cleaned her breast feathers and wings. Then she stuck her head under a wing and went to sleep.

George tried an experiment. He set Fox free. Instantly the little dog leaped at the pigeon, but Renni snapped at him so viciously that he darted back in fear. He came on again cautiously, with rapid waggling of his tail to show he had no evil intent and only wanted to play. But Renni was in no joking mood. He warned the terrier off and it was some time before he permitted him, now very humble and completely at a loss, to lie down beside him as he was used to do.

Undisturbed, the grey pigeon slept on.

From that day she stayed with Renni, sitting sometimes on his back, but generally on his head, not stirring from her perch even when he looked for the wounded. If this happened at night she might wake up but would soon go back to sleep.

Renni was so careful with her that he never really touched her. He was content to sniff at her and blow on her gently when he was at rest and the dove strolled back and forth between his forepaws.

Fox learned to put up with her presence. The pigeon treated him fearlessly and with a little condescension. She ignored his invitation to play. If he came too near she pecked him, and that was not very much to his liking. In the end he reached the point where he would have nothing to do with her.

If circumstances let the animals rest at night–of course they put in the days sleeping whenever they had the chance–they always presented the same picture. Renni lay stretched out on his side, Fox crouched down close against his breast, and the pigeon perched on his neck.

George did not interfere. "That's Renni's business and the dove's. I don't understand it, for I'm only a man." He smiled at his words and added: "But I must confess it pleases me to see animals friendly. It's a good sight even if I can't understand it. Indeed, it's strange what a charm things always have for you when you can't understand them—mighty strange."

Renni, Fox and the pigeon, that strangely assorted trio won a great deal of attention. Their reputation spread. Commissioned and non-commissioned officers and some of the men in the ranks came to get a quick look at them. With everyone Renni was friendly, gentle, reserved. Fox was so lively he made a nuisance of himself. The pigeon was very haughty. She took no notice whatever of human truck, and gave everyone to know that she was a lady of high social standing.

The soldiers laughed whenever these droll companions came into view. It was not the loud laughter that follows a joke. Nor was it at all the laugh of ridicule. It was rather an audible smile, a smile of cheerful approval. The sort of helpless smile you give when you see something strange and strangely appealing. The laugh you resort to before something you cannot explain, because you can think of nothing, nothing whatever, to say.

Even at the dressing-stations the surgeons would look up for a moment to give Renni and his pigeon a fleeting smile before they turned again to their grim and pressing work.

Chapter XXV

EVENTS TOOK THEM ONCE MORE TO the little town. They had won it back after a bitter struggle, and they found it far more forsaken and hopeless than before. They got a short rest here, for the troops had to recover from their weariness. The armoured cars and the heavy artillery moved out, supported by powerful squadrons of aircraft. The infantry kept in constant touch with them, ready to follow at any moment. It was now largely motorised. Even the Sanitary Corps had been provided with motor vehicles, and George and his animals could ride.

With the other dog-handlers he had his quarters in the roomy ground floor of the city hall. He got no pleasure from seeing the little town again. More houses were in ruins. The streets were full of debris. Signs of destruction were everywhere. The shops were all closed, for they had nothing left to sell. If one walked along the sidewalks, splinters of glass ground under the foot at every step, for there was none to sweep away the broken panes or all the other litter. It was very depressing.

With his first look George noted how terribly the number of people had shrunk. No children, no young boys and girls. Just the old women and a few old men. They slipped about pale and stricken, shabby, ragged, dirty. They seemed not to have washed for days and days. Some begged for bread, and if any got a piece, more would come hurrying up. George gave away as much as he could.

Fox, who always looked askance at anyone poorly dressed, barked and barked and raised a terrible row.

Renni, the pigeon perched on his head, would gaze at the people with the quiet kindliness characteristic of him. The poor folk were surprised at him and his companion, and in spite of their poverty, their timidity and fear, the glimmer of a smile would light their troubled faces.

George's gloom soon vanished. His personal work with the dead and the wounded, work carried to the point of utter exhaustion, had made him harder, more thick-skinned. Otherwise he could scarcely have endured the terrible experiences of war. He was, so to speak, not more than half-alive. He could not pull his thoughts together. He could not afford the relief of worry. So he became as unresponsive as a vegetable and looked forward only to the little satisfactions of the rest periods, of getting to his quarters, of eating and sleeping. It took the innocence of his animals to arouse emotion in him. Renni's confidence always touched him. His heart was moved by Fox's playful tricks. And he was still stirred by the strange way in which the dove had placed her trust in Renni.

• • •

When Nickel called out to him once, "Don't give all your bread away! These people are just pretending to be so poor to keep us from taking things from them!" George smiled and said, "Well, you hardly think they're millionaires, do you?"

He met three old acquaintances again, one right after the other. Accident often brings such meetings about, but these three cheered George enormously, because, coming so close together, they seemed to him arranged by a kindly Providence.

A corporal was marching by, stiff as a ramrod, with ferocity written on his face. He stopped before George, pointed to Renni and the pigeon, and snarled out, "Circus act?"

"Karl!" cried George. "I'm so glad to see you again!"

Ignoring his courtesy, Karl said mockingly, "Oh, so here you are! With the Brothers of Mercy, of course. Just like you! A real man would be fighting. Fighting!"

"Yes," George answered cheerfully, "but while he's fighting many a man is wounded, or maybe killed . . . so . . ."

Karl interrupted him, "What is to be will be, and that's all there is to it!"

"But you can't leave the wounded to die!"

A scornful gesture. "Nonsense! You're as soft-hearted as a pretty nurse!"

"Well, we have to have nurses, my dear Karl. And it doesn't hurt if they're pretty!"

"Perhaps. But I'm talking about men, not women. You're the same old milksop. You go to war and you don't even carry a gun!"

"Oh, yes I do!" George pointed to the pistol at his belt.

Karl touched the pistol with his finger. "Have you shot anybody yet?"

"Not so far."

"Well, I have! Plenty! I really couldn't tell you how many poor devils I've mowed down! Yes, old boy, a man like me is no such good-for-nothing as you!"

"Well, the best I can wish for you is that you'll never need the services of a good-for-nothing like me!"

"That's one thing I won't do! That would be a pretty picture, wouldn't it! When I fall, if I do, just leave me there! Don't disturb me. Just let me go!"

The conversation pained George and he tried to give it a different turn. "What's become of your Pasha?"

"He's done for!"

"Oh, I'm so sorry! How did it happen?"

"I don't feel sorry for the beast! He gave me too much worry!"

"Did he get sick?"

"Not he! Sound as a nut. But I couldn't take him into battle with me, and after all the trouble I'd had with the big cur . . . well, I just put a stop to it–and to him."

George felt ill, but made no comment.

Karl was plainly in a temper. He turned to go. "Say, are you going to try to make me believe you worked up this circus stunt without whipping?"

"I'm not trying to make you believe anything. And I never did try to. Not you! Nor anybody else!" George flared up. "I had nothing to do with that." He pointed to Renni and the pigeon.

All this time Renni had been looking off to one

side, perfectly indifferent. Fox held very still, though the hairs on his back stood stiff and straight.

Nickel put in his oar. "I can be witness to that. And so can all the rest of us. The friendship between Renni and the pigeon–no person had a hand in it."

Karl looked him over arrogantly. "Who asked you?" He saluted carelessly and went off.

"The big blowhard!" growled Nickel.

George too was angry. "He was always big-mouthed, always had a mean streak in him."

Nickel made a wry face. "I wouldn't be too sure about his courage."

"You're probably right there," smiled George.

"So, you know that side of him, do you?" said Nickel.

"I know a good many sides of him–all bad."

"Oh, ho!" Nickel slapped his thigh. "A coward! A dirty coward!"

"Well," George said, attempting to soften his words a little, "maybe he's brave enough. You never can tell. Fighting really ought to be his element. From the way he brags about it. . . ."

"Stop! Don't go on!" Nickel insisted. "A dirty coward is all that he is. You can tell it just by looking at him! He claims to be a hero. No, sir! A hero never brags."

And that was that.

After a while Renni got up, began swinging his tail faster and faster, and sniffing eagerly. Fox took his place by his side; he did not know what Renni was up to, but it looked like a greeting, so his stump of a tail started violently wagging.

It was the colonel. "There you are again!" he cried, coming to a halt with a whole group of officers around him. Renni was so enthusiastic that the pigeon on his head had to flap her wings to keep her balance. Fox smelled around at all the uniforms and seemed satisfied with what he found.

"How are you, Corporal?" said the colonel. He saluted the other dog-handlers, who, like George, stood stiffly at attention.

"What's this pigeon business?"

"Begging the Colonel's pardon, that's something that

just happened. She came along and adopted Renni, and now she never leaves him."

"Strange! . . . How about the fox terrier?"

"The poor little fellow, we found him in one of the houses. He's taken up with us and made friends, but he likes Renni better than me."

"Yes, that Renni!" said the colonel. "Good old Renni! "He stroked the dog who looked up at him with laughter in his eye. "Seems to me his girl friend's a bit jealous." He smiled, dodging the pigeon, who pecked angrily at his hand. "This dog's going to get you a whole menagerie, Corporal. Even animals trust him. That's easy to see. Does he act all right in war?"

"Perfectly, Colonel, perfectly."

The colonel shook his head. "A dog like that, gentlemen–it's simply amazing what a lot of good he can do. And quietly, without looking for thanks or reward, just as a matter of course. He's a real aid, a real rescuer. Last year during manœuvres, he got me out of a mighty tight hole. This fellow Renni is worth a dozen other dogs, aren't you, Renni?" He slapped him on the back. The pigeon did not understand this show of affection. Her neck stretched out and her wings lifted threateningly.

The colonel murmured, "Lo, the dove of peace!" and the officers laughed.

"Yes," he continued, "he's grateful and loyal to me, merely because he saved my life! All right, Renni, old man, we're friends, and friends we shall remain!" His hand stroked Renni's back. "It's a strange thing, gentlemen, it seems to be the same with dogs as with human beings. If you've saved a man's life, or helped him out of some bad fix, you stay attached to him forever, even though your loyalty makes a nuisance of you. No, no, partner, you're not a nuisance, of course not. I didn't mean you."

He turned to go. "Good-bye, Corporal! Good-bye, Renni! Good-bye, little Fox!"

A captain called to George, "Corporal, would you sell me your fox terrier?"

George saluted. "Just take him, Captain! I couldn't think of asking you anything for him!"

Fox was tied by a string. He refused to go, but the captain pulled him along, saying, "He'll soon grow used to me and get to like me. It's very nice of you to let me have him. I've wanted a dog for a long time."

Fox stood as firm as he could, ploughing along on all four legs as the captain pulled. Renni sent one short bark after him. Fox growled and whined.

The officers went off, talking together, and disappeared with Fox still struggling and holding back. Renni sat before his master and looked at him. He did not understand what had happened, and George thought that his look was reproachful. He seemed to be asking in his mute way, "How could you do a thing like that?" Or he might have been thinking, "I'd never have expected it of you!"

George was embarrassed, almost ashamed. He took Renni's muzzle in his hand. The pigeon tried to peck him. George felt so uncertain as he faced the two animals that he let go of Renni's head. "Renni, you know I couldn't refuse a captain," he excused himself. "I'm sorry about Fox, myself."

At the word Fox Renni growled. "It doesn't help

much that I'm as sorry about Fox as you are, does it? But when a captain asks for him, what can I do? I can't say no, can I?" Renni wagged his tail. "Please be in good humour with me, old fellow. Don't be cross!" Renni swung his plume faster. Cordial relations were restored.

"Don't look so down in the mouth," Nickel said, half in jest. He had been listening. "Renni's forgiven you."

George replied, "There was really nothing to forgive. What else could I do?"

"Well, then, why look so miserable?"

"Maybe that's how I feel. And no wonder, either! I didn't realise I was so attached to the little fellow. Now he's gone, I miss him."

"Of course you do. A man gets so fond of an animal like that . . . and what the colonel said about getting attached to anyone you've saved–well, that applies to you. You saved Fox, you know."

"Maybe so. But the way he held back and fought against going . . . his wretchedness . . . it hurts me to think of it."

"He'll have a pretty soft time with the captain, I imagine."

A soldier was standing at the bottom of the stairs looking up uncertainly, questioningly.

"Something you want?" Nickel asked. The man made no answer, but kept looking at George, who had turned and was about to go into the hall.

Then he called shyly, "Corporal! Oh, Corporal!"

"What is it?"

"Is it you, or isn't it?"

George replied, "Who are you, anyway?"

The soldier climbed the steps slowly, stood erect before George, and said in a low tone, "Flamingo is my name, Antony Flamingo. Perhaps the Corporal will remember . . ."

"Flamingo! Flamingo! Why, of course! I didn't recognise you at first!" George shook hands. "Please don't stand at attention. This isn't an official call, I hope. I'm surprised to see you. We haven't met in a long while—not since that day. Well, that's not our fault, it just happened so."

Flamingo, encouraged by this long speech, risked

the remark, "I had the honour of meeting you just that once, and I'll never forget it."

The slash he had given the poor man's face came back vividly to George's mind. Again he felt embarrassed. "How are you getting along?"

"I've never got along very well, and things are worse than ever now," Flamingo replied. "But I've given up expecting anything."

"How's your cute little spaniel?"

"My good old dog? Since that one time, I've never struck him. Not once. I swear it! I haven't that on my conscience."

"But what did you do with him?"

If Flamingo had spoken low and hesitantly before, now he fairly whispered. "I left him with my . . . my wife."

"So you married again?"

"Again? No." He dropped his eyes.

George tried to make it easier for him. "Did you send for her to come back?"

"No. . . . I didn't know where she was. She came of her own accord."

"Is that so?"

"Yes, just three weeks before I had to join my regiment. . . ."

"And you took her back?"

"Of course. What else could I do?"

"Certainly, certainly! We must always forgive those who repent."

Flamingo shook his head. "Repent? No, I don't think you'd say Amalie repented. Of course she said she was sorry . . . but I don't believe a word of it. She just ran out of money . . . and then she thought me good enough. . . ."

"And you left her at home?"

"Yes. Here I am in the war, and she's sitting snug back there. The three weeks we were together she was humble enough. She didn't have time to start making fun of me again, and . . ." He straightened up. "When I left she called me a hero! . . ." He burst out laughing. "Fine hero I am."

"Why not?" George tried to cheer him. "Maybe you are. You've been through several battles. . . ."

"Yes, and shook with fright every minute!"

"Don't be ashamed of that. The man who's afraid and fights on all the same—he's the brave man."

"But," said Flamingo, "I don't fight! I never fight! I shut both eyes every time I have to shoot." Suddenly he changed his tone. "My wife—she squandered my money, and she doesn't know I've saved up a lot more!" He winked knowingly. "I carry my bankbook with me. The account's in my name only. If I fall Amalie can have it, but not till I do. . . ."

"How will she treat the spaniel?"

"Fine! I'm sure of that. She was always good to the dog. . . . I was the only one she had it in for." He shrugged his shoulders. "God knows how it will all end, what with war out here and war back there!"

He started away, after a pitiful attempt at a salute. George and Nickel followed him with their eyes, as he went along, striving to show an energy he by no means possessed. Soon they lost sight of him in the crowds of soldiers.

"Poor specimen!" was Nickel's opinion.

"A fellow with no talent for happiness," said George

trying to soften his comrade's harsh judgment.

And then, suddenly, Fox was back with them again. He had slipped up very quietly, like a criminal coming home with a guilty conscience. No sooner had Renni caught sight of him than he leaped to meet him, jubilant, ready to celebrate. But Fox acted as though he were snapping at Renni's ear, while really he was whispering, "Be quiet!"

"Why?" Renni asked.

"I'm afraid He'll send me away again."

"Oh, no. He didn't want to give you up."

"Do you really think so?"

"I know it."

At that moment George ran his hand gently over Fox's head. "God bless you, little fellow! I'm so glad you're back with us!"

When he felt George's hand, a quiver of fear went over Fox, but as soon as he heard his voice, he went into a spasm of joy. He leaped up on George, on Renni. Like a whirlwind he rushed around among the soldiers who filled the space before the town hall. His yelps, barks and howls sounded now like cries of joy, now like sobs of grief, but they all amounted to this: "I won't stay any longer with that man who dragged me off. I'll never stay with him! If he carries me away again, I'll just run away again! How could anybody do a thing like that? Just as if I had no feelings! I was so hurt . . . so terribly hurt . . . and I was so homesick . . . for you, Renni . . . and for Him. . . ."

He ran around Renni pressing against him closely, caressingly. Renni waved his tail. Then Fox danced about George who tried to pet him.

"That'll do now," said Renni.

And George said, "All right, Fox . . . you're a fine boy . . . and you're back with me . . . and here's hoping you'll stay with me from now on in."

Panting, Fox threw himself down on the floor beside Renni. His tongue was hanging far out. When Renni lay down beside him and asked, "How did you ever manage to get loose?" Fox cut one eye around toward his string. It had been chewed in two and hung from his neck.

Man cannot read his fate. How then shall a little dog know where his safety lies?

Chapter XXVI

THE FIGHTING BEGAN AGAIN, wilder, more insane than ever. The earth shuddered from the crash of the heavy guns. The whistling shrieks of the grenades, the thundering explosions of bombs, the chatter of machine guns, the firing of armoured cars and tanks, all mingled in one raging, deafening clangour. Human voices could be heard above the stupendous din, but they sounded thin and pathetically faint. Sometimes they were cries of anguish or the gasp of the dying.

And again they were hoarse shouts of command, sharp, breathless, verging on panic and causing panic in those who heard.

Forward rolled the army. Forward . . . forward!

All the soldiers, all the officers seemed in a daze, in a sort of delirium, in which courage, horror and fear were so mingled that they could not be distinguished or separated.

They all had one common will, one common goal, one common irresistible impulse . . . to press onward.

The Sanitary Corps moved along in the rear of this flaming inferno, this huge engine of destruction. From the torn and trampled field which the army left them, they gleaned their sorrowful harvest. They had to go carefully about it, for sometimes enemy bombers flew overhead and sometimes long-range artillery swept the field.

But help must be brought where help was needed.

The number of hurt and injured was appalling. When at last one would have said that all must surely have been carried to the dressing-stations, the dogs would be sent out still again to find any that might by any possible chance have been overlooked. These must be helped at once if they were to be helped at all, for generally these were the most severely wounded, lying there unconscious, unable to make their presence known.

And then, as always, Renni did the best work. Not only was his skill superior but he seemed to be working by plan, with a definite purpose. In the whirlwind of his activity he would hardly notice the pigeon, who was constantly having to give up her favourite seat on his head for the safer one on his back. Nor did he bother with Fox, who ran along by his side or galloped ahead in busy idleness. George himself had reached the point where he hardly ever thought of Renni's companions. At first he had expected that the dove might bother Renni and Fox and distract his attention, but by now he had grown quite used to this animal comedy, as he called it. So now as Renni was not in the least disturbed by them, but rather performed his services more brilliantly than ever, George took a humorous view of terrier and pigeon.

And when the work was over—as long as the search was on both dog and master gave it complete absorption, and there was no time for joking—after the work was over, he would call the pigeon Renni's periscope, and Fox his no-account stooge.

One day Renni had found eleven unfortunates. It was growing late when George, a wagging tail on either side of him, went to the dressing-station with the last of the rescued. The sky was starless, and the night so inky black that the very din of the distant battle seemed hushed, extinguished. Only here and there the ray of a far-off searchlight would stab the heavens, to hunt for a wavering moment, and then even its climbing beam of light would disappear.

The work at the dressing-station ended, and the last of the ambulances was about to roll off to the field hospital.

George might have ridden in with one of them, like the other dog-trainers. But Renni seemed strangely uneasy. So he delayed. Nickel called to him, "Aren't you coming along?"

"No," George said shortly.

"You must be tired and hungry."

"Not especially," said George. "It's only a little way. I'd rather walk. It won't take much more than an hour."

So Nickel's ambulance went its way. George felt Renni pull impatiently on his leash. A sort of presentiment awoke in George, a foretaste of something disagreeable, painful. He thought: "If we should find another one . . . now . . . when all the stretcher-bearers have gone . . . when there isn't an ambulance left . . ." He thought it over: "Can Renni possibly have let one get by him . . . ? Strange! Worse than that–awful! The poor fellow would have to be in a dreadful state if even Renni could find no sign of life in him!"

He went on thinking and thinking, as he walked along the edge of the battlefield. He followed Renni's lead. The dog was testing the air in evident excitement. "Surely he'll soon find him now . . . but what will he find? And the wretched man will have to wait another hour till I get back with the ambulance . . . only he'll die first."

His thoughts were broken off short by Renni's sharp pull at the leash. Fox dashed ahead like a streak. George saw the little snow-white body flash through the dark, while he busied himself to free the now excited Renni from the leash.

All of a sudden two short quick barks rang out, with a queer sharpness in them. And immediately after a cry of pain, a shriek that died in a gurgle. Renni darted forward to Fox's rescue and George followed at a dead run.

As he ran he thought in half-conscious surprise: "That's no wounded man. That's something . . . something . . ."

He had about a hundred steps to go. Renni's bellow of rage gave wings to his feet. What went on there that made Renni charge like a mad dog, rush in, give way, and then attack again? He flicked on the flashlight which hung around his neck. The ray fell on a wildly distorted face. Two threatening eyes glared at him. The man reared up, deadly, menacing, right before him. A long thin-bladed knife gleamed in his uplifted hand, poised to strike.

Swift as lightning, George snatched at his pistol, fired once, twice, right at that wild and horrible face. It shuddered into something beyond recognition. The eyes glazed, went out. The man doubled up and, as he fell, he wavered out of the little circle of light into the enveloping darkness.

As quickly as it all happened, still George saw everything, from one fraction of a second to the next. Aghast, yet ready for danger, he bent over the fallen man.

He was dead. That blood-smeared face seemed to cry to heaven. "Most hideous of crimes!" flashed through George's mind. "A monster who robs the dead, who steals from the fallen . . . watches, rings, money . . . who murders the dying . . . with that knife."

He picked the knife up. The blade was ground to razor edge. A few feet away Renni broke into a long wailing howl of grief.

"Fox!" cried George, and reached him in one leap. He lay with a gaping wound in his side. Dead. Quite dead. Over his body stood Renni, mouth wide open, howling. The pigeon hovered restlessly on his back.

Shocked, shaken, George knelt by the dog's body. "Poor little Foxy! True and honest friend! No matter how many men have fallen, it is right for me to mourn for you."

Renni listened to his words with ears pricked up sharply. He understood and he echoed them with a melodious moaning, which gradually grew softer and softer. Now George spoke to him. "What do you say? We can't leave our old friend lying on the field? Let's bury him right here." As if to agree, Renni reached out one forepaw and laid it on his arm.

The same knife that had killed Fox helped dig his grave. "And it might have killed you, Renni, and me too," said George while he worked with it.

Renni looked on attentively. He had stopped his keening. On his back the pigeon had stuck her head under her wing. She was asleep. As George laid Fox's stiffening body in the hole, Renni gave one last low moan. He stood with nose pointing steeply downward and saw Fox disappear beneath the earth. George tamped the dirt carefully, and then, in sudden revulsion, he hurled the knife as far as he could into the dark.

"Come, Renni!"

They made for the field hospital, where they were to spend the night. They walked slowly, sadly. Renni's head was down, his tail hung limp. And as they walked, a vision of the man suddenly flared up in George's imagination—the man he'd shot, that dreadful, murderous face whose criminal fury had so suddenly broken, paled and sunk into the darkness. And George realised, "I've killed a man!"

Horror filled him. He defended himself to his rebellious conscience. "A hyena, a ghoul . . . ! And he killed Fox and tried to kill Renni and me. He would have done it too. I fired in self-defence." It was no use. Again and again the self-reproach returned: " . . . killed a man!"

When he tried to justify himself with the old saying, "All's fair in war," he found no comfort in it.

Reasoning like that might have justified the man he'd killed, might have led him to his gruesome crimes—the plea that he was only taking from the dead the things they'd never need again.

"Perhaps his children were hungry at home. . . . And I shot him down! It's my business to save men from death . . . and I have killed a man!"

He caught at Renni's collar. "You too, gentle Renni, your business is to help no less than mine—and you sprang at him in fury!"

But Renni, who usually responded to any words from his master, remained indifferent. He did not wag his tail. He just trotted quietly along.

George went on accusing himself. "How many wicked things I've done!" He thought of the blow he'd given poor, innocent Flamingo. A soft word would have been enough to stop his mad rage. There had been no call for brutal action.

And young Rupert Fifer. He wasn't all bad. He had just been led astray by hunger and poverty. Patient kindness would have brought him around. "What I should have done," thought George, "was try to awaken his better nature, train him in the right way. Patience and kindness! That's where I've failed. Completely. Beat him and throw him out of the house! Send him home sprawling! Make a young boy bitter forever. Kick him back into hopeless misery!"

And now this wretch who had sunk in war to the vilest of crimes . . . he should have shot to wound not to kill him, should have arrested him and taken him to the guard. But no . . . he had fired a bullet straight in his face. In blind rage he had willed to slaughter.

But was he fair to himself? Had there been time for choice?

So, in this wild agitation, he reached his quarters and went to bed, but could find no rest. Renni, who usually slept close against him, did not share his cot tonight, but stretched out beside it on the floor. He curled up there and, after whimpering softly, went to sleep.

Then Renni began to dream. And in his dream he saw the man again, the knife held high, and little Fox dead. He howled in high thin whines, and his legs twitched violently.

George tossed sleepless the whole night long. In the morning he told Nickel what had happened.

Nickel raged. "The beast, the unspeakable beast! A

bullet was too good for him. He ought to have been hanged! I tell you the best way to get rid of such vermin is the shortest way. String them up on the nearest tree! Hack them down without mercy! Ghouls like that violate the honoured dead who have given their lives for their country! There's no forgiveness for it! You were right, as right as rain! Execute them on the spot!" And he added, "Poor little Fox! Such a cute little fellow! It's a shame!"

At first the way Nickel took it touched and comforted George a little, but its effect did not last long. He did not dare speak of his self-accusations. He took especially good care of Renni, provided him with the best of food–though, indeed, Renni would scarcely touch it–stroked him, talked tenderly to him. The dog would wag his tail faintly, look at him with swift, sidelong glances, and drop his eyes to the ground.

"He's mourning for Fox," Nickel said gently.

George sighed. "Renni's tired of war . . . and I am too. . . ."

Chapter XXVII

BUT THE WAR WAS NOT OVER. NOT for a long time yet.

They had set up a new field hospital in an abandoned factory. The spacious rooms were filled with cots, and on every cot lay a wounded man. This one had his leg propped up; that, his arm in splints; a third, his head in a bandage. Many raved in fever. Many died, and they were carried out at once. Cries of agony or delirium rang through the halls, and an evil smell pervaded them in spite of the open windows.

Nurses hurried to and fro. They could not answer all the calls, the demands, the pleading. Most of them showed care and kindness; only a few seemed peevish. Surgeons repeatedly made their rounds.

George and Renni, who were stationed here, came in one evening when their work was done for the time being, and spent a couple of days at the hospital. George made himself useful in every way he could think of.

Renni had gradually regained cheerfulness, and he tried to win George back to it, but without success.

Once Renni followed George into a ward. The wounded lay quiet, hardly stirring. They had fallen prey to the apathy that is apt to overcome those who are long ill or long confined. A sort of indifference to their own condition, and to passing time. A sort of daze which may go over into oblivion. But the sight of Renni with the pigeon on his head aroused even the most benumbed. It amused and cheered them all.

"You mustn't come in here, Renni," whispered George. "Wait outside."

But Renni had no idea of waiting outside. The men

called to him from all sides, and on all sides asked George his name. Renni brightened the whole room. The nurses smiled and let him stay. Even the surgeons made no objection. Some petted him—and the dog took it forbearingly.

Renni went steadily from bed to bed, searching, sniffing, drawing away from hands that sought to stroke or stop him. At last he paused before a certain cot, sat down on his hind quarters, and looked carefully at the man who lay there, his face bright with fever.

He was an enemy soldier, a strapping peasant boy. He opened his eyes.

"What's that perched there on your skull?" he asked the dog.

A nurse whispered to George, "We have to be awfully careful with this patient. Shot through the lungs. Terrible case of pneumonia."

"Renni!" cried George at once. But Renni, instead of springing at his master's word, refused to budge an inch.

"Well, after all," said the nurse, "he's beyond hurting or helping. He won't live longer than tomorrow morning, at the most. Leave your dog with him. It might give him one last pleasure."

So George did not repeat his command, but instead questioned the nurse about the sick boy.

"He's always asking for cigarettes," she said, "but they're strictly forbidden. So is meat, and coffee. He's allowed nothing but milk . . . and he won't drink that. He keeps asking for cigarettes, meat and coffee over and over. He fairly pleads for them!"

"Poor devil!" said George. Renni seemed of the same opinion, for he laid one forepaw on the edge of the bed.

"You're mighty friendly with me," said the wounded soldier. Renni's tail swung faster. The boy went on in a hoarse voice, "Everybody here is nice to me . . . it's hard to believe I'm among enemies. But you, you're especially nice. Pity you haven't a cigarette. I'll bet you'd give me one."

As George went out he heard his invitation to Renni: "Come see me every day . . . do you hear? Every day."

The nurse whispered sympathetically, "Every day . . . that won't be very many days."

From beds near by patients began tossing cigarettes to the poor soldier. Young peasants like him, foes yesterday, comrades now in pain and distress, they took pity on their fellow sufferer and cared not a fig for the doctor's stern commands. He smoked happily, eagerly. He smoked as one dying of thirst might cool his throat at a clear spring. And later he smoked again, occasionally, hurriedly, at odd moments when nurses and doctors weren't around, just a few blissful puffs. And doing it thus secretly gave him exquisite pleasure. He did not die that day, nor the next, nor the day after. His fever was still high, but he was cheerful. Every day Renni would sit down by his bed and stay there even when George was busy elsewhere–in the kitchen, the sterilising room, or the operating room.

Once when he came back he said to the nurse, "I don't understand it. The man has something in him, or Renni wouldn't have taken such a fancy to him. I like him a lot too."

"We're all very fond of him," the nurse said in a low tone. "It's inconceivable how he goes on living."

The surgeon came in unexpectedly with three nurses. They had to examine a man severely wounded who should have had an amputation before this but had steadfastly refused. A little distance away Renni sat happily by his peasant boy, one paw on the edge of the bed and the pigeon as usual on his head. The surgeon and the nurses kept trying to persuade their patient to have his leg off. Suddenly Renni gave one short, loud bark. Just one. It sounded like an alarm, and startled everyone. The surgeon jumped. "What's the matter here?" he shouted irritably.

The nurse in charge called out, "The foreigner is dying," and hurried toward him. From the blanket that covered him, just about where his stomach was, a thin blue column of smoke was rising.

"No!" cried the nurse, taken aback. "No! He's smoking!"

The surgeon, coming over with the other nurses, tore off the covers. The foreigner lay very quiet, not saying a word and a cigarette was in his fingers. When he saw them come into the ward, he had quickly hidden the cigarette under the blanket. It had burned a hole in the blanket, and only Renni's bark had saved him from serious trouble. But it had also got him caught in the act. So there he lay, with never a word. Caught! What could he say? The doctor laughed. The nurses laughed. Laughter spread from cot to cot, through the whole great room. And at last the culprit himself began laughing, put the cigarette to his lips and blew a great puff into the air. As cool as a cucumber. Renni started to run back and forth along the rows of cots, overjoyed to have been of help.

"I'll send you a packet of cigarettes," the doctor decided. "You may smoke as much as you please." He turned to the supervisor. "All my orders are cancelled. You may let him have meat and coffee." Then with a smile he added, "It won't hurt him. He's going to get well."

The enemy soldier smiled also. He murmured, "Of course I'll get well! At last . . . now you've found the proper treatment!"

Chapter XXVIII

THAT NIGHT RENNI AND GEORGE were ordered back to duty. They made their way to the field which had been the scene of the latest battle and which they had to search. A countryside covered with bushes which stretched away clear to a forest's edge. Here their "gleaning" was very complicated. The Medical Corps had finished their work, but it was assumed that there might be still some few fallen men lying in the brush, or, if they had been able to crawl away in the shell-torn woods where they sought safety and where it would be hard to find them.

If they were still alive, they'd be expecting help. Without dogs it would be quite impossible to find them. Stretcher-bearers and ambulances stood ready and waiting. A small detachment of military police were on hand, for, since George's experience with the robber, it had been thought necessary to keep strict watch over forsaken corners of the battlefield.

Renni sniffed the air and ran off at once. George could not see him at any distance, even with his flash-light. When he came back George called him off. They waited for the first pale gleam of dawn, and soon enough were able to see. Renni went eagerly to work again. He promptly rummaged up three wounded men in the bushes. George whistled for the stretcher-bearers, and everything went off in regular order. There was no one left in the brush, but Renni found one more, unconscious, in the open meadow. That seemed to end the job.

But no. Renni stopped stiff, and sniffed excitedly toward the forest. Right! The woods!

It was not easy to get through them. Broken trunks of trees, shot down by artillery, in falling had become entangled with the undergrowth, and their matted tops blocked the way. Renni found three more wounded here. The bearers with much difficulty reached them, and with still more difficulty got them out of the woods.

Renni hunted on. He crawled into the thickest underbrush following a scent. As George fought his difficult way after him, he heard a feeble voice. "At last . . . Thank God!"

George reached the man.

Who should be lying there but Karl? He was flat on his back, stretched out at full-length, very pale, his face distorted in a painful grimace, and his weary eyes brimming with tears.

"You poor fellow . . ." George cried.

"Yes. I'm badly hurt. . . . Thank God you've come," moaned Karl.

"Where are you hit?"

"In the hip, the right one . . . mortal wound . . ."

George bent over and looked at the spot. "A flesh

wound," he thought, "not very dangerous. If it were he could hardly go on talking at that rate."

"Haven't you any sort of stimulant?"

Greedily he swallowed the cognac George gave him.

Renni sat by him on his haunches, waving his tail. Karl said, "Fine old dog. . . . You fellows from the Sanitary Corps . . . you have been my only hope . . . for hours . . . I've been lying here for hours . . . helpless . . . despairing!"

"Why didn't you call for help?"

"How could I? I hadn't the strength. You see how weak I am. Besides, I did call . . . I bellowed . . . and no one heard me."

George thought to himself, "He probably fell asleep," and started to go for a stretcher.

"Stay with me, please," begged Karl. "Oh, please don't leave me alone."

George signalled with his whistle.

"These dogs are a blessing." Karl reached out a hand to Renni, but when the dog avoided it, he let it sink as if he had no strength left in him.

He made trouble for the bearers. He groaned pitifully

whenever they touched him. First he'd tell them what to do, then he'd correct them, and then he'd praise them. When they lifted him onto the stretcher, he gave a cry of pain which to George's ear seemed not quite genuine. When they were all in the ambulance, George and Renni included, he said gloomily and as if to himself, "Well, I suppose it's 'good-bye, fair world' for me."

George did not answer. He recalled Karl's boasting–how he had said, "If I fall, just let me lie"–his contempt for the Sanitary Corps, and Nickel's accurate appraisal of the man. Then Karl spoke directly to him: "Will I die? . . . Hide nothing from me! I'm strong enough to hear the worst. . . ."

George felt like saying, "You poor excuse for a man, you deserve an earful."

But he shook his head as he answered, "No, certainly not. Of course not! I'm no doctor, but if my experience counts for anything, you can be back at the front in four or five weeks."

Karl cried out violently, "Nonsense! You're crazy! I don't want to! I won't! I've had enough war!"

"Well," George thought, "that's once he's been honest," but he made no comment.

At Karl's wail, Renni, who had been lying on the floor, reared on his haunches, pricked up his ears, and, without a wag of his tail, looked with sleepy contempt into this face that had unmasked itself.

Chapter XXIX

DAYS OF BATTLE LENGTHENED into weeks, and weeks into months. Short periods of rest, and then into the service again.

The Sanitary Corps had to work beyond their strength when the army retreated, and retreat was now more often the order of the day. The search grew much more difficult and had to be done more and more hurriedly. George and Renni had spells when they were numb and dazed, and went through their tasks as mechanically as robots.

The dog got over this more quickly than his master. He could sleep at any time, even if it were only for a moment or two. He would lie down, close his eyes, and at once drop into slumber that freed him from the awful present. When he awoke, he acted more cheerful and refreshed. He was awake all over in an instant, flashing to complete life and activity the moment his eyes opened.

It was not so easy for his master. All he saw on the battlefield–the blood and wounds, the torment and agony–gave his eyes and his nerves no rest, even when they might have rested, and so his exhaustion grew. He got even less sleep than was allotted him. He would walk about, drunk for sleep, with all his consciousness focussed in one longing, the longing for a bed. Beyond this, nothing. Everything else gone. But even so, subconsciously he was always waiting for the call to duty, in a tension that did not permit him to relax.

When at last terrific weariness overwhelmed him, he plunged into a gulf of leaden slumber, from which he awakened slowly and had to fight his way back to reality.

He stood one morning after the night's search was ended, waiting for the ambulance to take him and the dog back to the barracks at the field hospital. The sky hung low, gloomy. Heavy rain clouds were driven along by a cutting wind. George was freezing, Renni shivered, for it was late in the autumn.

The road where they were standing ran hard by the edge of a forest. On the other side an open field spread out which had been the scene of battle. A few dead were still lying there. George and Renni turned their eyes from them to the woods where yellow leaves were whirling. But mostly they watched the road full of troops, troops as far as the eye could see. If ever there was a break in the ranks, a clear space, George would lift his gaze to the next detachment coming up; otherwise he might miss the ambulance. Now the cannon rumbled and thundered along.

"We must wait, old man," said George. "We're not important now."

Renni waved his tail gently. He had heard few words like these for some time. Their relations had not changed. It was only that both of them were so worn out. The bond between them was known only by action, not by words. George was always concerned for Renni, looking after his food, his water, and above all his safety. Renni hung on George's every accent, look and gesture. He knew what even the slightest meant. But to exchange tender words and caresses, the mind must be freer of worry and one must have more time. They were never free from worry. They had never a moment to themselves.

Now they watched the endless column march by, only half-realising that they watched it. Why didn't the ambulance come to take them to their rest, the rest that would be so pitifully short?

A machine-gun company passed slowly. Every horse was loaded with a gun and an ammunition chest. They went in a shambling trot, their low-hung heads rising and falling as they stepped. They went on, offering up the pitiful remnant of their strength, hungry, sleepy, patient . . . and brave. Alongside marched the soldiers, hungry, sleepy, patient, and as brave. The horses had no faintest idea of what the war was about, why they were being tortured. And except for their orders, the soldiers were no better off.

A horse dropped out of the ranks and stopped. He could go no farther. The soldiers knew it instantly. Things like that had happened before. Two of them sprang forward, if their heavy haste could be called "springing." They took down the machine gun, eased it to the ground at the edge of the road. They unharnessed the horse, stripping it of bridle, leather pouches, ammunition chest. They were very quiet about their work. The horse waited submissively until they were through, as though a silent communion passed between him and the men.

He stood there for a few seconds, free of all his trappings, free from service, from all duty and all torturing effort.

The column moved on. Not a look, not a call, not

a word of farewell for the dying animal. But you felt a sort of shyness in those men.

Renni ran to the horse, sniffed, wagged his tail, tried to reach the drooping lips. But the horse, in its weariness, paid no attention. It turned toward the meadow, dragging one foot after the other farther and farther into the grass. At last it stopped. That dragging gait and now that still, gaunt figure were like things seen in a dream.

A slight quiver through the wasted body–and all was over.

George thought, "He gave all he had–to the last brcath."

The next evening George and Renni were "gleaning" in a wood far from this meadow. It had poured all day long, and still the fighting had gone on. Now the evening sky showed blue and the sinking sun painted a rainbow. But George did not see the beauty to which he had always been so alive. He did not feel the peace which hovered in the air. That very air had been but now the scene of murderous battles—like the soft earth, like the cool depths of the sea. Peace nowhere! Nowhere peace! All he felt was a feeble satisfaction that the rain no longer dripped on him, that he was done with searching over the wet ground in a wet coat. Now the "gleaning" only made him weary, bored him. There was a time when it had been full of shocks. But everything loses the keen edge of its hurt, even for a man as sensitive as George. Even dreadful things fade in their dreadfulness, and monotony breeds indifference to the horrors of warfare. The mighty, dramatic struggle, constantly repeated, ends by losing more and more of its power to appall.

War drives everything noble, everything spiritual, out of the heart, grinds it to a kind of dullness, makes it capable of inflicting frightful destruction without emotion, and capable of watching the ruin with as little feeling.

When George hurried along behind Renni in the work of mercy, he thought of Karl's words, "What is to be will be, and that's all there is to it!" Something in him tried to agree with them. But then he felt ashamed to face his dog. Renni went as eagerly about his task as on the first day. His interest, his sympathy, his will power, his care in searching had not slackened in the least. No matter how exhausted, how hungry, how sleepy he might be, call him to work and he would wag his tail, leap forward and do with perfection all he was supposed to do. George was upheld by this example. Renni shamed him, spurred him on, brought him face to face with his better self.

So he loved his brave dog more than ever. If he failed to show it, or showed it but seldom and briefly, it was because no word or gesture could express his overwhelming love. Any caress would be empty and futile. Spare the effort, save the little energy it would take, for the absorbing job.

Renni also economised his energy, responsive to his master's mood. His signs of affection became rarer, too, more sparing.

But he watched George all the time, guessed a second beforehand what he wanted, what he meant to do, and was the first to move.

On this calm evening Renni ran in the underbrush under the shattered trees, sniffing with nose to the ground. The pigeon, unable to hold onto his lowered head, had shifted to his back. He ran swiftly, zigzagging, veering suddenly, his legs and body spattered with wet earth. George hurried after him, boots splashing through mudholes. He would think, "Why do they pick this mud to wallow in?" and then, ashamed, but more on Renni's account than from conviction, he would add, "The poor fellows!"

Renni had already found six, and George had sent them back to the first-aid station. This forest bore fruit.

It was growing very dark. Under the trees it was full twilight. George decided the search for this night was about over, and he and Renni made ready to go back. All at once the dog threw his head up, sniffed, took a few steps in an uncertain circle, tested the air again, and scurried through the brush toward a distant clearing. The pigeon on his back kept waving her wings. George was not particularly interested and followed without hurry. But Renni was very much in earnest.

When he reached the wounded man, George started.

"Flamingo!" he cried, kneeling down. "Is it you, Antony?"

Flamingo opened his eyes and smiled, "Yes." His voice was very low. "I'm so glad someone I know . . . with me . . ." His voice failed. He made an effort and went on, "Oh, it's nothing. . . . Don't . . . don't bother with me . . ."

George tried to comfort him. "Why, we'll have you in a nice clean bed in a jiffy, and your pain will be over."

"Pain? I have no pain." Flamingo smiled. "I'm free, freer than I've been for a long time . . . freer . . . and happier . . . more at peace."

George put his whistle to his lips.

"What are you going to do?"

"I'm going to call the men to take you out of here. I'll stay with you till they come."

"Just leave me. . . . Don't worry about me. . . . I'm all right. Others need you more than I . . . others worse wounded . . . they need you more."

His eyes followed Renni. He stopped talking. His

lips moved as though he were panting. And suddenly he was dead.

George tenderly closed his eyes. Then he waved to Renni, who had moved quietly over to one side, and walked softly away, saying to himself, "You too . . . all you had . . . to the last breath."

Chapter XXX

A LATER DAY FOUND THEM ON A broad, spreading field, with little hillocks in it like waves rising and falling. Only a few hours before it had been ploughed, trampled, torn by a furious battle. The men of the Sanitary Corps ran with their stretchers to the ambulances, hurried back, fetching scores of wounded. George and Renni stood ready, waiting their turn. A stretcher was carried close past them. Their old friend, the colonel, lay on it. Renni waved his tail in greeting.

"Well, Renni, they found me without you this time!" cried the colonel. "I got caught this time, Corporal."

George stepped forward. The bearers stopped. "I hope it isn't bad, Colonel."

"Bad luck is bad luck!" His face was suddenly wrenched in pain. "My leg again, and the ankle again, too! A bad wound! And it hurts like blazes!"

"I'm sure the Colonel will soon be well again."

"Yes, if God's willing. But a cripple likely, hobbling around."

Renni crowded against the litter. He was beside himself with joy over the meeting.

"Wait a bit, Renni, wait a bit! Wait till I can crawl around and get rid of this pain! Then we'll have a frolic. All right, boys, forward march! Good-bye, Corporal. Good-bye, Renni. I'll be seeing you soon."

George saluted and the bearers went on. Renni wanted to run after them.

"Easy, boy, easy," George quieted him. "The colonel doesn't need you. You're right to love him as much as you do. A good man! A real man! Pity he couldn't get home from this war without a scratch."

It took a long while to clear this field. George and Renni had a wearisome time to wait. "They'll find them all today," said George. "There won't be anything left for us to do."

Renni swung his plume, looked up at his master as though he were begging, "May I? Let me!" He kept lifting, first one forepaw, then the other, a sort of dance in one spot. The pigeon balanced on his head.

At last came the command, "Go!"

The dog ran swiftly forward, drew small circles then larger ones, stopped to try the air, whirled around to follow a scent, gave it up, struck another trace.

Now Renni found a man hidden in low brush. He sniffed, scratched at the small bushes, made sure of his find, and started back to fetch George.

The man greeted them with a laugh. "I never saw anything so comical in my life as that dog and that bird. I had to go and get wounded to see a thing like that!"

"Yes, a pigeon . . ." George said without thinking.

The man drew down the corners of his mouth. "Think I mistook her for an eagle? Don't tell me a pigeon's not a bird!" He went on talking at a clip. "*Columba,* the dove. My dear fellow, I am a schoolteacher! Every little snot-nose knows a dove when he sees one. But it's so startling to see that double-decker partnership, especially when . . ."

George broke in: "You're pretty brisk but . . ."

The other took no notice of the interruption. ". . . especially when a man is lying here as I am. . . ." He straightened up painfully. "What I mean is . . . I called as loud as I could . . . I fairly bawled . . . but nobody heard me. You fellows must have cotton in your ears. It's scandalous! If it hadn't been for the dog . . . and the pigeon . . ." He laughed again. "This is the first time I ever saw one of these Red Cross dogs. I didn't know anything about them. Do they all have pigeons on their heads?"

"I must go now," George said resolutely. "I must arrange to have you taken back! Wait ten minutes, and they'll be here."

Ever afterward George could remember what happened then, but only in fragments, mistily, like a fantastic dream.

A heavy shell bored its way into the ground and exploded. The rush of its fall could be plainly heard, but panic fear left no telling which way to run.

It fell perhaps a hundred paces from where George stood. Like the bursting of a volcano, earth, dust and smoke towered to the sky. Steel splinters whizzed in every direction. Under the hail of clods and steel George saw Renni collapse and fall. Horrified, desperate, he screamed, "Renni! Renni!"

At that instant he felt a blow on the shoulder, as if someone had struck him with a club. He fell, and went unconscious. He did not see the pigeon rise from Renni's head and fly away.

When he awoke, he looked around bewildered, dazed. Where was he?

A small, snow-white room. A snow-white bed. Everything smelling of ether. Someone in a snow-white gown bending over him. It was the surgeon, the one no longer young, who had recognised Renni when he reported at the beginning of the war. But George did not recognise him now.

"Well," the surgeon smiled in a friendly way, "the operation's over."

"Operation?" George was more fully awake. He tried to raise himself, but a blaze of pain in his shoulder stopped him.

"Be as quiet as you can! You mustn't . . ."

George wouldn't let him finish. "Where's my dog?" he stammered, "my dog . . . my . . . ?"

"Keep cool! Here he is! Right here . . . beside your bed. You couldn't see him because you can't move. But call him and he'll come."

A sharp nose rose over the edge of the bed.

"Renni!" whispered George, "dear, good old Renni. Come up here. I want to see your face."

"He can't do that . . . not yet."

"Are you wounded, Renni? You too?" George asked anxiously. "Are you badly hurt, friend? Where are you hit?"

The doctor answered for the dog. "A stone caught

him on the upper leg . . . the bone's injured. I had to bandage a small open wound. Nothing serious. You're far harder hit, Corporal."

"Thank God!" sighed George.

"Now go to sleep!" the surgeon ordered.

George tried to say something.

"No. Don't argue! Go to sleep! You *must* sleep! You need sleep now. We'll talk later."

He left the room. George whispered, "Good old boy . . . my Renni . . . you're still alive!" Then he fell asleep. A deep, dreamless sleep fell upon him like a benediction. Hours later he awoke with his mind perfectly clear. The surgeon was again at his bedside.

"How are you?"

All George said was, "Where's my dog?"

"He's all right. What about you?"

"I want to see him. Renni! Renni!"

Again the sharp nose thrust up over the edge of the bed. George tried to put out his hand, but could not. The pain in his shoulder went through him like a dagger.

"Is his nose cold or hot?"

"It's begun to get cooler, and it will be wet again before long. He's getting well faster than you are, Corporal."

"Why did you have to operate on me?"

"You had a splinter from that shell sticking in your shoulder. It had to come out."

"Really? What all happened? I don't know a thing about it, you know."

"Sergeant-Major Nickel found you. Just after that crazy shell burst. Nobody else dared go in there. They were afraid more of them would be sent over."

"Nickel?"

"Yes. He heard the dog howl. He kept howling for someone to come. Nickel knew his voice, it seems. The dog couldn't move, but his nose pointed to where you were. You were covered with earth. You had passed out. We couldn't wait till you came to. Besides . . ." The surgeon paused.

"Besides?" repeated George.

"Well, they brought you in, and your friend Nickel spoke to you. You sort of woke up, half-way, but only for a few seconds, and you were out of your head. So we . . . we took the necessary steps immediately."

"Necessary . . . ?"

"Yes. The shot for tetanus. Then the anaesthetic and the operation, all at the same time."

George thought for a moment. Nickel . . . brave man . . . good friend. "Where is Nickel now?"

"He was ordered away early this morning."

"Too bad, too bad! Who knows when I'll get to see him again."

"Oh, you'll see him all right."

"But something might happen to him."

"Nothing's going to happen to him."

"But, say! Where's that pigeon Renni had? What became of her?"

The surgeon shrugged. "I've no idea."

"Do you hear, Renni? Your pigeon's gone."

Once more Renni's muzzle came over the edge of the bed, and a slight tapping told that he wagged his tail.

"Anything else?" asked the surgeon.

"Yes, one thing more." George thought again. "If I remember, I was with a wounded man . . . a jolly fellow. . . . Who brought him in? . . . And how's he getting along?"

"He's past suffering. A shell splinter struck him in the head."

"Poor chap! He was so gay, not a bit worried over his wound."

When the surgeon left, a pretty young nurse brought in some warm milk. A glass for George, a bowl for the dog. Renni, who had been used to this for some days, began to lap loudly. When George started drinking, he realised he was hungry. It was the first food he had had.

"Thank you," he said, and gave back the empty glass. The nurse smiled and pointed at Renni. "He likes it."

"So do I," said George. He thought a moment, and then went on, "There's one thing I don't understand. I've a room all to myself, and the dog's allowed to stay with me. How does that happen?"

The nurse smiled in friendly fashion. "Our staff surgeon ordered it."

"Such a favour. . . . After all I'm only a corporal . . . Why?"

"The staff surgeon is a man first, a soldier after." She smiled in a still warmer way. "He thinks your distinguished services deserve distinguished treatment. And we're all of his opinion! We think it's wonderful of him to give the dog medical treatment himself, instead of calling a vet."

"He . . . himself . . . the staff surgeon?"

"Don't be so surprised, Corporal. The surgeon's right. He says this dog has done so much for so many men, let men do something for him."

"Was there a great deal to do for Renni?"

"Quite a lot."

"Nurse, do you know . . . is there a colonel here? . . ."

"With a wound in his ankle? Yes, and he's going to get well soon. Corporal, do you remember that enemy soldier who loved your dog so?"

"Why, of course. The fellow who wanted a smoke. Did he die?"

"Oh, no, he's perfectly well. Before we moved here, we sent him to the prison camp."

"A prisoner? But he was so friendly with everyone!"

The nurse smiled. "It's a rule of the game."

"Rule?" George shook his head. "In this man's war, they don't stick much to rules."

In a few days he could sit up in bed with a support at his back. He could look Renni in the face now, could see those clear, bright eyes whose gaze rested tenderly, trustingly on him. Through the nights and through the days they had both slept, master and dog alike, sometimes dreamlessly, sometimes oppressed by the terrible visions which spread before them, the confused and ghastly panorama of their war experience. Often George had been awakened by the peculiar high-pitched, choking cry that Renni gave in his sleep.

"How much longer have I got to stay here in the hospital?" George asked the surgeon.

"Two or three weeks. Can't say exactly yet. But don't let that worry you. When you get well, you're going home."

"Home!" George was astounded.

"Certainly. You're no longer fit for active duty. Nor

your dog, either." The surgeon pointed to Renni, who had come limping to meet him and stood waving his tail, his left hind leg drawn up tightly against his body. "He has found and saved his full share. He can't do more of that, not with his wounded leg. Oh, it will get better in time, much better, but never quite the way it was!"

George dropped his head in a sudden fear. "How about me? Am I going to be a cripple too?"

"Not a bit of it." The doctor's denial was emphatic and convincing. "Don't go fancying any such nonsense! You're going to be as well as anybody. But, you know, there's quite a difference between the hardships of war and your duties at home!"

Home! Home! It began to come back to George that he had a home.

The word sang through his soul like a ravishing melody. Home! To go home!

Out of the dreary waste of gory images that had blinded him to every part of his real self, images which he now thrust resolutely from him, there gradually arose, in his memory and his hope, a host of lovely scenes . . . the garden, the fields, the house . . . Mother . . . Tanya, beautiful Tanya.

Renni was trying harder and harder to get into bed with him. The nurse, watching his vain efforts, asked, "Does that bother you?"

"Oh, nurse," was the answer, "I would be as happy to have him at my side as he would be to get here."

She understood, and helped the dog onto the bed. Renni was mad with joy. But even so, he shielded his lame leg, and he was careful about his wounded master. So there he lay, pressed close against George, washing his hands and face, tapping the bedclothes with his waving plume.

"We're going home, Renni! Home! Know what that means, to be home again?" He said the words slowly and carefully to him, "Mother . . . Tanya . . . Kitty! We'll be seeing our friends–Vogg . . . and Bettina . . . and Vladimir." At each name Renni's ears went up, he gave a little happy whine, and his tail wagged so it sounded like a drum.

The two of them spent long, peaceful days together

on the bed. Eager yearning, pain growing less and less.

The war went on, somewhere in the distance. But for them, dog and master, it was over. They had done their duty as far as they could, had even shed their blood. Now they were free to go home.

Free!

Now with clear conscience they could yield to their natural, peaceful longings. They could forget the horror–or try their best to forget.

War had given them back the right to think of their nearest and dearest. The future was open, paid for by all they had done and all they had suffered. They two together.

George could never think of life without Renni. They had been united from the first, in their play, in their training, through deadly dangers, through all the work of rescue, through all the pain they had shared.

So now as the hours passed and George repeated softly, ten, twenty times, "Home! Mother! Mother!" Renni shared his joy. He would lift his beautiful head from George's breast as often as his sharp ears went up to catch the words.

Indeed, he raised his head even when George just thought "Mother" to himself.

And in Renni's innocent eyes shone the visible reflection of loyal hope, clear for all to read, the hope which flowed like a stream through George's being. And the same stream warmed the dog's heart too.

Adventure takes flight when Pegasus lands in New York City.

"A WINNING MIX OF MODERN ADVENTURE AND CLASSIC FANTASY."

—Rick Riordan, author of the Percy Jackson & the Olympians series

EBOOK EDITIONS ALSO AVAILABLE

FROM ALADDIN

KIDS.SIMONANDSCHUSTER.COM

If you like horses, you'll love these books:

You and Your Horse

Misty of Chincoteague

King of the Wind

Justin Morgan Had a Horse

Take the Reins

Chasing Blue

Behind the Bit

Triple Fault

Best Enemies

Little White Lies

Rival Revenge

Home Sweet Drama

FROM ALADDIN

PUBLISHED BY SIMON & SCHUSTER